PICKLES vs. THE ZOMBIES

PICKLES vs. THE ZOMBIES

BY ANGELA MISRI

DCB

Canada Council for the Arts **Conseil des Arts du Canada** ONTARIO ARTS COUNCIL CONSEIL DES ARTS DE L'ONTARIO an Ontario government agency un organisme du gouvernement de l'Ontario

 ONTARIO CREATES | ONTARIO CRÉATIF ▌◆▌ Canadian Heritage Patrimoine canadien Canadä

The publisher gratefully acknowledges the support of the Canada Council
for the Arts and the Ontario Arts Council for its publishing program. We
acknowledge the financial support of the Government of Canada through the
Canada Book Fund (CBF) for our publishing activities, and the Government of
Ontario through Ontario Creates, an agency of the Ontario Ministry of Culture,
and the Ontario Book Publishing Tax Credit Program.

LIBRARY AND ARCHIVES CANADA CATALOGUING IN PUBLICATION

Title: Pickles vs. the zombies / Angela Misri.
Other titles: Pickles versus the zombies
Names: Misri, Angela, author.
Identifiers: Canadiana (print) 20190089652 |
Canadiana (ebook) 20190089660 |
ISBN 9781770865587 (softcover) | ISBN 9781770865594 (HTML)
Classification: LCC PS8626.I824 P53 2019 | DDC jC813/.6—dc23

United States Library of Congress Control Number: 2018967101

Cover art: Emma Dolan
Interior text design: tannicegdesigns.ca

Printed and bound in Canada.
Manufactured by Friesens in Altona, Manitoba, Canada in August 2019.

DCB
AN IMPRINT OF CORMORANT BOOKS INC.
260 Spadina Avenue, Suite 502, Toronto, ON M5T 2E4
www.dcbyoungreaders.com
www.cormorantbooks.com

For Kenzie

PICKLES vs. THE ZOMBIES

DAY ONE

I watched the era of human domination end from a sun-dappled window seat.

In hindsight, I should have taken it more seriously, but as a predator I was more curious than afraid. Also, I'm an indoor cat who watches way too much TV. My tolerance for dramatic violence might be a little messed up.

"Wally, wake up," I said, poking the fat, gray mass at my side with my paw.

"Huh?" Wally mumbled, hauling himself to attention. Wally was from a family of military cats; his prized possession was the bronze general's star on his collar he'd inherited from his father. Wally's mother was none other than the spy Von Paws. Yes, THAT Von Paws. Sadly, Wally was also an indoor cat, so he had never actually gone to war, something that bugged him to no end.

At this point, you're probably wondering what resplendent family tree I descended from. Well, sorry to disappoint, but like 75% of the housecat population, I have no clue who my parents are. My first memory is of rolling around in a glass cage with five other calico kittens who looked identical to me, down to the black freckles on our noses. I drank my first drop of milk from a latex nipple attached to the cage, and when I left on my current assignment, I didn't even have a name for the other cats to call out to say goodbye.

My pet and I were born the same week, and I was assigned to this home when we were both eight weeks old. I was Connor's second word after "mama" and he was my first love and only family. Unless you counted Generalissimo Wally.

"Those three humans are eating an old human," I reported, my own eyes fixed on the bloody scene below.

Wally yawned, stretched, and finally turned his face to the street. "So?" he snapped. "Weaker gets eaten by stronger. Circle of life, Pickles. How many times do I have to explain it to you?"

"This is different," I said, pressing myself against the glass. "There's something wrong with the predator humans. They're not talking. And they're moving around super weirdly."

Wally snorted. "Humans are terrible predators. What

you're seeing there is pack mentality. Obviously those three humans have dogs as owners. Poor monkeys."

The three predator humans were shuffling away from their prey now, leaving behind a mess of people parts and a walker.

"They're so slow, it's a wonder they could catch anything to eat."

"The prey was very old," I said.

"Mmm," Wally said, lowering himself back to his sleeping position. "Wake me up when the pets get home. I need to remind the male to clean the litter."

I nodded, my eyes still on the newly quiet suburban street, watching as the leaves in the trees blew softly in the wind. I could hear no birdsong, and even the squirrels seemed to be taking a break from their incessant travels. It was the end of the human workday, but other than the attack we had just witnessed, I had seen no other humans in hours.

My pet was due home from the daycare soon, so I curled into a ball to rest. Connor was two and always needed my help to settle down when he got home. It was the busiest time of day for me, and I took my assignment seriously.

DAY TWO

"They're not going to come home any faster with this drama," Wally called as I flew by him on the way to the back door.

Still nothing. No sign of my pet or Wally's.

I whipped back to the front door where my partner was cleaning himself, rubbing his paw over his whiskers repeatedly. Describing Wally as a long-haired cat was an insult to hair, because surely he had enough hair follicles on his rotund body to supply three cats and a small toupee. In the summer, our pets would have to take him in to be shorn like the world's smallest, toothiest sheep, lest he start running into walls, unable to see through his fringe of Sia-like bangs.

I stood at the front door, glaring at it. "The sun is down, the moon is up, and they're still not home."

"Stand down, soldier," Wally replied, checking the star on his collar for shine. He rubbed his paw over it repeatedly until it sparkled the way it was supposed to. "They probably went on one of those human-only trips. It's not on my schedule, but they are terrible at updating me on their movements."

I am a short-haired calico, which, according to Wally, gave me a starting rank of Private. Wally gave me a thorough once-over as I stood at attention every morning. Every whisker and eyebrow hair was analyzed and adjusted to meet his exacting standards. I was pretty sure all promotions were based on growing hair as long and thick as his. So, I was going to be a Private forever.

"Relax, girl. Go read a book or something," Wally said, turning away and stalking to our shared food dish. "The pets will be home soon."

DAY THREE

"It's been three days," Wally whined plaintively.

"You know there's no one here to see you but me, right?" I replied without looking at him. I was back at the window seat, watching the street.

There had been another flurry of activity moments ago, with one of the groaning humans taking a beating from a pack of other humans. The "winning" human pack hadn't eaten their adversary, though. Perhaps it was just an expression of dominance on their part ... like the sparrow I had threatened through the back window yesterday. I'm pretty sure she understood my hiss, even through the glass. Wally says most birds will drop dead of fright before taking on a real cat. I don't know that he's right about that, but I prefer a panel of glass between us just in case.

"This is unbearable," Wally repeated, rolling around on the floor in mock-agony, "a standing army must have provisions."

I rolled my eyes but was careful to keep my back to him, and not to show any disrespect. Wally had lived here for many years; his pets were the parents of mine. I owed him much for my training. Plus, I didn't want to be demoted to whatever was below a Private.

"Uh oh," I hissed, standing up.

"What?" demanded Wally from the floor.

I didn't need to answer, though, as the object of my concern bounded up onto the roof, slowly walking towards the window where I now stood at the ready.

"Well, look who's people-watching," Ginger said, sitting on his haunches and trying to look casual. An orange tabby with very long whiskers and eyelashes, Ginger had white paws that looked like slouchy rolled-down human socks, a genetic feature he loved to take credit for, as if he picked his feet out of a Gap catalogue.

"Get lost, riffraff," Wally said, landing beside me with more grace than usual.

"Or what?" Ginger replied, eyeing the slightly open window. It would be a squeeze for me to edge through to reach the orange-haired cat on the other side, but he didn't need to know that.

"Just scram, Ginger," I said, slipping my paw through the space under the window to demonstrate my intention.

"Hey, I just came up here to get a view of the zombies," Ginger replied, turning his back to us and slowly walking away. Every move this cat made looked like he was posing on a literal catwalk. As if photographers followed his every move.

"The what?" I blurted out, hating myself the second the question left my lips.

Ginger turned around, his smirk wide. "The zombies. You know, the dead humans wandering the streets, eating anything that moves."

"Never heard of 'em," said Wally, but his ears (and mine) were pointed directly at Ginger.

"Zombies?" I repeated. I looked at the bookshelf behind us. Where had I read about zombies? Or had I seen them on TV? I spent most of my reading time immersed in graphic novels and manga.

"Maybe your pets don't have a name for them, but mine do," Ginger replied, sitting down to examine his claws, an action that usually got Wally's back up.

Not today, though.

"Zombies eh?" Wally repeated, trying the word out himself. "Are they a new kind of human?"

Ginger rolled his eyes dramatically. "They're not new, they're just dead."

"So, this isn't just what happens to humans when

they die?" I asked. I'd never witnessed a human death before.

"No," Wally said before Ginger could answer. "My pet's father died before you were assigned, Pickles. He died, got stiff, never moved again. I got a good look at him before he was discovered."

Wally turned his attention back to the fluffy orange cat on the other side of the glass. "What makes you say they're dead?"

"The smell, for starters," Ginger answered, crinkling his pink nose for emphasis. "And the fact that they're impossible to kill."

Wally snorted. "Nothing's impossible to kill."

Ginger sat back down on our roof as if he had all the time in the world. "You watch. That zombie down there — he'll get back up."

I fixed my eyes on the still figure in the road, ignoring Wally's repeated snorts.

Minutes ticked by, but cats are patient: we watch.

Our patience was rewarded. The zombie began to stir, and I took an involuntary step backwards. Even Wally was amazed. The man's two arms had been lost in the battle we'd witnessed, but somehow, he pulled himself to his feet, silent but for the groans of his battered body.

"Well, I'll be a long-haired Siamese," said Wally through his teeth. We were all up, our tails twitching as the zombie slouched away, his movements as unnatural as the body that still moved.

I turned wide eyes towards Wally, new worries forming in my head. "Where is Connor?"

DAY FIVE

"**S**tuffing yourself is a bad idea," I said, watching Wally eat the food scattered on the floor.

It had taken some tearing and ripping, but we had managed to release the food from its canvas container this morning. There was now food scattered all over the basement floor, and Wally seemed to be doing his best to gather it all into the safety of his stomach.

I had gone through book after book looking for where I had come across the word *zombie*, but had found nothing. I was sure it was from a TV show. One Wally's pets watched after Connor was in bed, usually with me curled up next to him.

"Wally …," I started to say, but a noise above us interrupted me.

"The pets!" I exclaimed, bounding away and taking the stairs two at a time. Wally was calling for me to stop, but I hadn't scented my pet in days and I was too excited to slow down.

I careened around the corner into the kitchen to stop suddenly in front of three humans I had never sniffed before.

My ears flattened as they all turned towards me, their arms raised in aggression.

"It's just a cat," one said, lowering his weapon slowly.

"How do we know it's not a zombie cat?" another demanded, advancing on my position.

Part of me wanted to run away (okay, let's be honest here, most of me wanted to run away), but Wally was beside me, so I followed his lead and made myself as big and intimidating as I could.

"There are no zombie cats," the third said, returning to his looting, placing cans of our pets' food in his backpack. Wally hissed at the pack of humans, who ignored him, focusing instead on their nefarious deed. They were worse than raccoons, looting and stealing our pets' food.

"Pickles, count everything they take," hissed Wally from beside me, "we will at least report our losses if we can't stop them, I swear it."

From the messages flying off his whiskers, Wally was

about to jump onto the counter and take a swipe at the nearest human when the first thief pulled out of one of Connor's little juice boxes. That was low, to steal from a baby animal. I growled low in my throat to warn him to put it back down.

"I hope the kid got out okay," he said, his eyes sad as he held the small box in his hand.

I felt a chill run down my spine. Did he know something about my pet?

The other two humans stopped their scavenging at his softly spoken words.

"The whole family is probably lying low till we hear something on the radio."

"Hear what?" I hissed. "Where is my pet?"

They ignored me, their language skills as limited as their eyesight.

"We might even meet them on the road," said the human, replacing the juice box in the cupboard and hefting his backpack.

They turned and walked past me, their bags full of our food, and it was only at the back door that the sad one locked eyes with me. He bent down and unlocked the cat door, pushing it so it swung, showing me our backyard. Then he was gone.

DAY EIGHT

"This is pointless."

"What's pointless?" asked Ginger from outside on the windowsill. He'd been quietly watching us try to turn on the radio for the past ten minutes, and we had done our best to ignore him.

"We have to find out where Connor is, and those thieves said the radio would tell us," I answered, knocking the black rectangle controller to the floor. Radios were human contraptions, sometimes filling our house with tonally questionable music. Wally claimed to enjoy something he called "jazz," but its chief attraction seemed to be that it put him and his pet to sleep within minutes in the recliner, leaving us with their loud, matching snores.

"Why are you here?" Wally demanded, stalking to the window, his tail twitching.

"Boooooored," Ginger answered, rubbing himself against the windowsill and scenting it. "Nothing to do at home. Nothing on TV. So bored."

"Stop that!" commanded Wally. "This is not your territory. The borders are well-marked. Private Pickles, make a note."

Ginger wasn't listening, though. He had turned towards the back fence, where two humans pawed in a vain attempt to gain entry.

Suddenly a new zombie appeared, entering the yard from the corner, groaning and slouching alarmingly quickly towards Ginger, whose back arched like a furry stegosaurus. This zombie I recognized. He used to be called Vish, and he used to care for Connor when the parents were away. Now ... he was in no condition to care for anyone.

We could hear Ginger's hissing through the cat door, filled with dire warnings and threats, but the once-Vish ignored them all, continuing to advance on the orange cat.

Dead humans behind him, a dead human gnashing his teeth mere yards away, Ginger reacted at the same time I realized his intent, scrambling through our cat door and into our house with all the grace of a pug walking a balance beam.

"What is wrong with you?" hissed Wally, his eyes locked on the humans, but his words entirely for the invading cat.

"What did you expect me to do?" he hissed back, all three of us now lined up in a row of hissing, arched anger, our teeth bared at the young dead human on the other side of the glass. The two other zombies had pushed down the back fence and groaned their way to the once-Vish where he pawed at the door. I was more scared than I had ever been in my life and it was this stupid orange cat's fault.

"You led them right to us," I said through my chattering teeth.

"Yeah, because they totally missed you before," Ginger replied, anger and fear evident in the twitch of his tail.

But the humans seemed confused by the door, pressing against it but making no move to turn the handle.

"What are they waiting for?" Wally demanded, his eyes switching between the shambling, groaning threats.

"I … don't think they remember how to open doors," I said, as surprised as Wally at their clumsiness. I was sure we were done for.

They spent a few more minutes vainly slamming their bodies against the door and glass and then turned to leave, one at a time, their expressions vacant.

We stood there, tense, unwilling to believe that they would give up so easily.

I was scared to unlock my limbs. Afraid I would collapse onto the floor like some kind of liquid cat and never re-form into a solid.

Predictably, it was Ginger who relaxed first, easing out of his aggressive stance to sit back on the rectangular controller on the floor.

A buzz of static made all three of us jump as the radio came on.

"By the Saber!" Wally cursed, his voice high and surprised.

"Shh!" I replied, willing my heart to stop hammering in my ears and positioning myself right next to the speaker. "I hear humans!"

DAY NINE

"Are you sure?" I asked for the last time.

Wally nodded solemnly from his position at the window. "I won't leave this post undefended."

My stomach roiled at the thought of leaving my partner behind, of venturing out into the world outside my home without Wally leading the way, but the radio said the humans were to meet at the local hospital. My heart told me that Connor needed me, and he was my number one responsibility. I needed to know he was safe. Besides, the inside of the house was proving almost as unpredictable as the outside.

Sensing my hesitation, Wally smiled through his teeth. "It is right that you seek out your pet, Pickles. He is young and vulnerable. I will wait here until you return."

"He's only two," I said, miserable at being forced into this choice. "He's entirely dependent on his parents."

"And you," Wally put in.

I nodded, trying to act more sure of myself than I was. "With these dead humans roving freely, I have to make sure he's all right. We'll go to the hospital and come right back."

"So ... are we going or not?" Ginger called from the floor, where he was unceremoniously stretched out. "I'm getting bored again."

"I still don't like the idea of you traveling with such an unscrupulous furball ..."

"Hey, I can hear you, you know!"

"... but it seems to be our only choice," Wally finished, scenting my left side as he spoke. "This is a scouting mission, Private; find out what you can and return quickly."

I nodded, trying not to throw up. I followed Ginger as he gave a saucy wink to Wally and then squeezed out through the window opening. He stepped out onto our roof and then leapt across to Cinnamon's, where he looked back at me impatiently. This was the moment. I looked at the space between my house and the next roof and it seemed to warp and grow too big to leap across. I felt the wind ruffle my fur, an entirely different feeling from the warmth of the furnace, and the light out here was so much brighter than through a window. Could I do this? I had to do this. I had to know Connor was safe.

I took one last look at Wally through the glass and then took a deep breath before I leapt to Ginger's side.

It was the last time I'd see Wally for a very long time.

"Cinnamon's been missing for days," Ginger explained. "I've looked in every window, and seen no sign of her."

Cinnamon was a thin Tonkinese cat I had only really interacted with through glass. As neither of us were outdoor cats, we'd never spoken, but her tail often transmitted scathing messages about the borders between her house and ours that sent Wally into a tizzy. If a squirrel scampered from a tree in our backyard into hers, she blamed us. If a bird dared poop on her flowers and not ours, she blamed us. I really hoped she didn't fly into a tail-twitching frenzy at my brief use of her rooftop.

Ginger was leaping as he talked, barely stopping between houses. I'd never done this before, so I had trouble keeping up. The rooftops were made of an odd material I'd never felt under my paws before. And they were hot. Like my window seat under direct sunlight, but harder and scratchier in texture.

We leapt from rooftop to rooftop until the end of the block, Ginger punctuating each landing with a description of the inhabitants. I wasn't sure if he was showing off his worldliness or filling the quiet so as to cover his nervousness. Even an outdoor cat like Ginger had a limit to his comfortable range. As an indoor cat, this was both terrifying and exhilarating. There was so much to see, so much I didn't know. Every step away from the house brought new questions to mind. What kinds of birds were those? Were there really that many kinds of leaves? What was that smell? What was THAT smell?

"I still don't know why you're coming with me," I said as I tried not to stare at a family of chipmunks wrestling a huge shoe into their home in a tree.

Ginger shrugged nonchalantly before answering, always trying to seem cooler than he was. "Could be an adventure, could be a bust. Whatever. Gotta have something to talk about to the neighborhood mammals, right?"

I shook my head behind his back. This cat was all about the attention.

"A hamster named Emmy and two dogs named Ralph and Vance live here," he said, pressing up against the window to peer inside. I took a moment to clean my paw of leaf bits. Outdoor living is messier, that's for sure.

"See anyone?" I asked.

Other than the incessant birds chirping at the sky as if it were a normal spring day, not the fall of an empire, we had seen no other animals.

"Nah, but the hamster is restricted to its pet's bedroom, so I don't expect ...."

Ginger was interrupted by the sudden appearance of a large dog's head rising to look at us from the window we had been peering through.

Ginger leapt backwards instinctively.

"What do you want, male feline?" demanded the mastiff.

"You're alive," Ginger said, not moving from the safety of his position.

"Barely," the mastiff answered with a growl. "What are you doing on my roof?"

"What do you mean 'barely'?" I asked instead, coming forward despite Ginger's twitching whiskers and their clear message to keep my distance. I'd seen this dog walking his pets around the neighborhood, but this was the closest we'd ever been. He really was gigantic.

The dog looked over his huge shoulder and then back our way. "The pets have gone mad, female feline. They've been trying to get in this room for a week. I've not slept in days."

"Where's Vance?" Ginger asked from behind me.

"I'm Vance, you dumb alley cat," he growled with a shake of his head. "Ralph is gone. Went down fighting. Saved Emmy. She survived, but she fled and I haven't heard a peep from her since." He howled his sadness at the room. I flinched at the sound. I'd never seen a hamster before in my life, but I could feel this dog's sadness at her loss all the way through the glass.

By now I was close enough to the window to see into the sunroom, and I could see the door had been barricaded with some chairs tipped on their sides.

"That keeps the humans out?" I asked, running my eyes over the large dog, stopping on the large bitemark on his back.

"They've gone mad," Vance repeated, licking his lips again. "They have forgotten the simplest of activities. Even how to open doors. Or to recognize loyal friends."

"You've been bitten," I remarked, unable to keep the tremor out of my voice, but feeling Ginger take another step back on the roof.

"Ay, female feline," Vance replied. "By my own pet. Just one bite. Though it seems to be enough."

I tilted my head in question.

"It's like a venom in my blood," he explained, turning in a circle before sitting down, a slight whine entering his voice. "I can't eat, I'm shivering with cold, and I'm weak as a newborn pup."

"We should go," Ginger said from behind me. I turned around to see what had got his back up; two shuffling zombies were making their way down the street towards us. They hadn't seen us yet, but their unnatural sounds made it hard to concentrate.

Vance put two giant paws against the window and I leapt back. "Go! Before they catch you. Don't let them bite you, and for the Great Wolf's Hide, female feline, don't bite them."

I nodded, I really wanted to ask what would happen if I bit one, but Ginger was leaving, his nervousness stoking mine. I followed Ginger as he scampered off the roof and into the branches of the nearest tree. I forced myself not to look back.

DAY TEN

"Are you sure this is the right way?"

"The radio told the humans to meet at the hospital."

I nodded, my fur upsettingly damp and dirty from our night under a trashcan. Another first for me. I napped in the sun of my window seat and slept the night away next to Connor, warm and comfortable. I never knew how good I had it. How did outdoor mammals stand this?

"My pet was a healer. I know how to get to the hospital, I followed him to work twice a week," said Ginger, who somehow still looked clean enough to audition for a Meow Mix commercial.

We were in yet another alleyway, picking our way through the garbage and dead animals, and I was doing my best to ignore the smells of death.

Hundreds of dead rodents littered the alley, their mouths red with the blood that had poisoned them. Had they died after biting a zombie? Or were they eating other animals and were soon to turn into zombies themselves?

Three large rats crouched over something that had once been alive and wore sneakers, arguing about the spoils, but when I called out to warn them of the dangers of eating these defiled bodies, they scattered to their secretive holes in the walls. No rats had ever dared enter our home, so I had never met one, let alone killed one. Wally would talk about his grand adventure with a rat that got trapped in a wall one summer when he was a kitten, but even then, there was no confrontation between cat and rat. The rat found his way out of the wall and never returned.

"Don't bother," Ginger said, leaping from the large garbage bin up and onto a metal staircase.

"Will they die, or turn into zombies themselves?" I asked, mimicking Ginger's ascent up the stairs, not liking the way the cold metal felt under my paws, or the clicking sound our claws made and seemed to resonate around the alley.

I watched his orange shoulders shrug before he spoke.

"There's so little meat on a rodent that I don't expect it's ever come up. They'd just be a few mouthfuls for a human. But the only zombies I've seen were human. I don't think animals turn into zombies."

I thought this over as we negotiated our way up two more floors of staircases. "And what about Vance?"

"Don't know," Ginger replied. "Don't especially care."

I didn't understand that. How could you not care? I barely knew Vance and I cared. Heck, I even cared about the missing hamster, Emmy.

We had reached the flat pebbled roof by now, where Ginger pointed triumphantly to a huge building in the distance.

"There. That big building with the cross," he said.

"That's the hospital?" I said, trying not to betray my nervousness. It was so far away and there were so many buildings between us. This entire journey "outside" was basically a trip from one human-made box to this other human-made box. How did humans make so many huge stone boxes? And why?

"That's where my pet works," he answered.

"Then that's where we'll find Connor," I said, focusing on my purpose. This adventure was almost over. Thank the Saber.

"I CAN KEEP going," I said, my tail twitching as I spoke, my eyes fixed on our goal.

"Well, I can't," Ginger answered. "I'm starving and I'm tired and I need a bath." He grumpily batted at a foul-smelling cigarette butt. I'd never understand the humans who put them in their mouths, inhaling their nasty smoke. Ginger said it was like catnip for humans, but catnip smells marvelous. Not like these dead weeds.

My stomach growled in response, but I ignored it, walking to the edge of the staircase to look out at the street.

We had made our way leaping across rooftops if they were close enough, and making the more arduous descent and ascent of the metal staircases if the roofs were not close enough. We couldn't get through doors because of the handles, something cat paws were not made to manipulate. I could sometimes open doors at home that had the long handles, if I leaned on them with both paws, but the round handles were impossible. If Connor was on the other side of that kind of handle, I'd have to meow at the door until one of Wally's pets let me in. All of this up and down travel was a tiring business, but I was determined to make it to our goal. Walking through the streets directly was more dangerous, as bands of roaming zombies could (and did) appear at any turn.

Looking back over how far we had come, I marveled at it. The human world was a maze of streets and lanes, lined with buildings, some tall with hundreds of windows, some squat and ugly, something that I'd never given much thought to in my past life as an indoor cat. How many humans were there in this city? And how many were still alive?

"There, I see an open window two floors down," Ginger said, immediately vaulting in that direction. I followed, my eyes scanning for movement inside the apartments. Ginger stuck his face under the open window, taking a big sniff.

"Feline?" I asked, hopefully.

"Feline," he confirmed before shimmying under the window. "Hopefully we'll find some allies."

But a search of the small apartment yielded no one, human or feline. The food in the dish was a few days old, but neither of us cared. We finished it in minutes and then I collapsed under a couch with a sigh, feeling safe for the first time since we left Wally and my lovely house.

DAY ELEVEN

I woke up to a thud at the window. I bounced to my feet, hearing Ginger do the same behind me.

A very fat raccoon was struggling his way into the apartment through the half open window.

"Well? Don't just stand there gawking," he hissed at us. "Help me!"

I glanced at Ginger, who shrugged. His disregard for all other beings was starting to grate on me. Slowly, I made my way to the window. "Who's chasing you?" I demanded, trying to see behind the raccoon's girth.

The fat mammal was now spinning, trying to negotiate its way in by whatever angle worked. I hopped up next to him, not close enough to be grabbed by his clever paws, but near enough to see a few eagles in the lightening sky.

"Come ON," he said, sucking in his belly fat.

I looked down at Ginger. "What should we do?"

"How do I know?" Ginger replied.

I hated that Wally wasn't here. What do I know about raccoons? I'd only ever encountered them through a pane of glass as they invaded our pets' garbage bins. The eagles screeched again and I jumped back. The raccoon wrapped a paw around the window, trying to push it up. I couldn't let him die like this, could I?

"Hey! Look at those paws!" I said, looking at the raccoon's paw as he flexed his fingers around the window. "I bet he could open the human doors at the hospital."

"Huh?" answered the raccoon, his masked eyes flicking between us and the eagles through the window.

"Could come in handy," Ginger nodded with a grin, understanding. "You're going to owe us, raccoon, if we help you."

One of the eagles gave a screech that set all of our teeth on edge. No matter where you sat on the food chain, that sound made you want to dive under the covers.

The raccoon was sweating now, freaking out, so I held out a paw. "Say it."

"I owe you, yes, please, my oath," he blathered, his paws extended my way.

I grabbed both his paws with mine and leapt to the floor ... and hung ... in mid-air. Even my added weight didn't dislodge him.

"Ginger!" I yelled, seeing the eagle making his dive, sensing our vulnerability.

Then Ginger pounced right on the raccoon's belly, deflating it enough to tumble us to the floor in a heap of fur and whiskers. Ginger flipped mid-air, but the raccoon howled, and held me to his chest like a scared kid with a teddy bear as he fell. The eagle hit the window with a bang and screeched some very creative cuss words at us as he pecked at the window.

I extricated myself from the pile of raccoon as gracefully as I could, immediately relocating to beside the orange cat on the table nearby.

Ginger was already licking himself clean and started on me as soon as I was in reach. Normally, I would have hissed at him, but being hugged by a raccoon was totally gross, so I allowed the very personal bathing to my ears and cheeks while I took care of my paws.

Meanwhile the raccoon was huffing on the floor, running his paws all over himself as if to make sure all his parts were still attached.

"Holy biscuits, that was close!" he said, finally rolling from his back to his front and then onto his ample backside to stare at us. "You guys! Seriously! I was almost bird feed!"

"That eagle was crazy," Ginger agreed. "I doubt he could have lifted you."

"Didn't need to lift me to tear me apart, did he?" the raccoon answered with a shudder that ran all the way down his striped tail. He pulled at his black whiskers as he spoke, a nervous habit, I guessed.

"Are they scavengers?" I asked, staring at the eagle who had given up pecking at the window and took to the sky with one last insult about our fathers. "Couldn't they take their pick of the dead animals on the streets?"

"No one is safe scavenging these days," the raccoon said, hooking one of his paws towards the window. "You must have seen the trail of rat bodies below."

We both nodded, and then sat there, awkwardly looking at each other.

"So ... you got any food?"

"THE HOSPITAL IS tricky," Trip said, his mouth full of Cheetos.

The raccoon was a font of information once you got some food in him. He'd told us what felt like his entire life story, from how he'd earned the name Trip (exactly how you'd imagine) to losing his pack/gaze to eagles and zombies. Or at least that's what he thought happened. The truth was, he'd fallen asleep one morning with his gaze of raccoons, and when he woke up that night, he was alone. Ginger communicated his interpretation of that story through his whiskers, and I couldn't disagree. This raccoon was a series of unfortunate events, most of which seemed to originate with his innate clumsiness. But he was the first raccoon I'd ever spoken to, and that was pretty cool.

"I was there yesterday, in the bins," he said, licking his powdered fingertips with a sucking sound that made me a little nauseated. "The doors have handles and they're very heavy."

"But you've seen humans going in," I pressed him, desperate to believe Connor was safe inside.

"Affirmative, pretty kitty cat!" he said, stuffing more Cheetos into his face. "And the live kind, not the dead kind. Though there are plenty of the walking dead between us and the hospital."

"I think we should go now," Ginger said from the window, where he had been watching for the eagles to come back, "in daylight."

Trip looked back and forth between us before giving the half-finished bag of Cheetos a forlorn look.

"Once you get us into the hospital you can come right back here," I said, leaping up to the window to Ginger's side.

"I've never seen a kitty as pretty as you," said Trip, holding up his orange dusted paw for comparison. "Orange and white and gray and black. You're like a buffet of pretty colors!"

Cats are basically colorblind, but we can see shades of colors, so I know I have a coat of many shades, and I know that Ginger's main shade is called orange, like the patches on my ears.

That said, being called a "buffet" in this age of dead humans that ate anything that moved was not a compliment.

"Here, help me," Ginger said, putting his shoulder under the window and slowly standing up. Together we managed to open the window another five inches so that Trip could slide out more easily.

He led the way up the metal staircase to the roof, sniffing the air and watching the sky for the dreaded eagles. We crossed the roof single file and reached the edge of the building.

"Uh oh," whispered Trip, staring down between the buildings. The hospital had no external metal staircase, just a flat glass side. I looked at the alley between us and wasn't surprised to see bands of roving zombies pacing back and forth.

"Are those your bins?" I asked, pointing at the large containers in the alley below.

"Yup, humans throw out all kinds of tasty things. It's why so many raccoons live in the city," Trip said, pulling at his whiskers, "though yesterday those bins didn't have quite so many dead humans circling them."

"I'm starting to feel like this adventure is exceeding the value of the story I will tell," Ginger said, pacing along the edge of our building.

I squinted across the rooftops. "Wait, do you see that vent?"

Trip stopped pulling at his whiskers, "Yeah! Good one! You could slink down the vents from the roof."

"You mean 'we,' right raccoon?" Ginger said, looking at the vents too now.

"Ha!" Trip laughed and then lost his smile, "You're kidding, right cats? How would I ever get to that roof top?"

Instead of answering with words, Ginger backed up, measured wind resistance with his whiskers, and launched himself into the air, landing neatly on the roof of the hospital.

I grinned at him, "Easy peasy, nip and cheesy!" Once I'd seen it done, I knew I could do it too.

"I can't do that!" Trip said, aghast.

I leapt before Trip was finished speaking, landing perfectly beside Ginger and then giving him one of his patented twirls like I was posing for the cameras.

"Yes, you can!" I called. My paws were itching to find Connor now, he was so close. And then we'd be home before Wally had a chance to miss scolding me.

"No, I can't!" Trip replied, backing up more. "I can't!"

"You owe us, raccoon," Ginger hissed, his ears flattening against his head. "We have many doors ahead of us that we can't open."

"I can't, I can't." Trip was gibbering, and I felt my patience ebbing away as Trip and Ginger argued. I was ready to let the raccoon go at this point. He was becoming more trouble than he was worth. I walked over to the vent, sure I would hear Connor's voice echoing up through the pipes. We wouldn't need a raccoon. Humans would open the doors for us because the humans made the doors. A long coil of rope, some lumber, and several human tools sat beside the vent. More stuff to build with, humans really never stopped changing the outside world to suit them. I put my two front paws on the vent and stuck my head in. All I could hear was mechanical clunking sounds.

Disappointed, I pulled my head back out just in time to hear the screech of an eagle.

"Pickles!" I heard Ginger yell as I flattened instinctively. The gravel of the roof was hard and cold under my cheek as I felt the talons of the bird pass within an inch of my shoulders.

I rolled to the side and dove under the pile of lumber, listening to the eagle screech. That bird had the vocabulary of a drunk seagull! Ginger squeezed in right beside me, so we were staring out at the opposite roof, our hearts hammering in unison as we watched Trip scramble. Correction, this is the most scared I'd ever been in my life.

"He's got no cover," Ginger hissed.

"We have to help him," I replied, wincing as Trip nearly fell off the roof dodging the eagles as they dove and screeched.

My eyes lit on the rope and I got an idea. "It's crazy," I said to myself. "Completely crazy. Ginger will never go for it."

"Look for cover, you ridiculous raccoon," Ginger yelled, his claws coming out in frustration.

"Here, help me," I said to him, zipping out of our hiding place to grab one end of the rope. The eagles didn't seem to notice, they were so focused on their prey. I was back under the lumber in a flash.

"Find a way to secure this, it needs to support Trip," I said, spitting out the rope at Ginger's feet.

He gaped up at me, but I didn't give either of us time to think about it. I zipped back out onto the roof, grabbed the other end of the rope, and leapt across the alleyway to the opposite roof.

I landed badly, the adrenaline and fear making me skid across the rooftop, drawing the attention of the fowl creatures circling above.

"Trip!" I yelled, running straight at him as he scurried here and there. "Grab this and follow me."

Somehow, he understood my words despite the rope

in my mouth, and he chomped on the rope as I ran by. I dropped the rope as soon as he had it and led the way to the edge of the roof. I looked back once. "You have to jump!" I yelled, and then I was airborne again.

I turned mid-air to watch Trip leap over the edge of the building, an eagle arcing down towards him.

He wasn't even close.

Trip fell, his masked eyes wide and I prayed to the Saber that I hadn't just killed him.

The rope went taut beside me with a "sproing" sound and I heard the raccoon hit the side of the building with a splat. The whole thing would have been kind of comical if not for the death-from-above birds that continued to screech inappropriate things about our litter processes.

I raced to the edge, calling down, "Trip! Climb!"

Trip shook his head to clear it and did exactly that, using those skillful paws of his to climb hand over hand up towards me. It wasn't going to be enough. What else could I do? I looked at the sky and hissed, leading the birds away with my catcalls.

"Hey! Feather brains!" I yelled, zipping all around, under the lumber, behind the vents, loving the humans for all this convenient cover out here in nature, "Stupid dodos! Beeeeeee-agles!"

They screeched their curses at me, but I dipped and dodged as fast as I could, somehow staying clear of their deadly talons until I saw Trip sprint by on all fours and throw himself into the vent.

Ginger raced in after him, calling for me as I hurled myself in behind them, hoping for a soft landing, even if that ended up being a rotund raccoon.

DAY TWELVE

"We're going in circles," Ginger declared finally, sitting down at a junction of three tunnels.

I wanted to disagree but was far too tired. It seemed like days since we'd rolled and slid down the ducts to this level. Trip said humans used these vents to move air around the building — cold in the summer, warm in the winter. We were in the ceiling of the building, that much we could tell because every hundred yards or so along the duct a vent with slits would appear and we'd all crowd around and peer into the hallway below. So far, every time we did that all we'd see were groaning, shuffling zombies.

Trip was suffering the most; he had to squeeze and

squish his body through these tight spaces, but he wasn't complaining at all.

I sat down over a vent, peering down to see a number on a door: "Seven hundred eighty-five. You're right Ginger, we're going in circles."

Trip leaned back against the wall of the duct, the most relaxed position he could find in such close quarters.

"We should rest here," I suggested, taking pity on the larger animal. "Trip, why don't you lie down flat there. We can fit over on this side of the duct; the rest is yours."

Trip started to do that, gingerly spreading out to full width until that part of the metal duct was entirely filled with raccoon. He sighed with relief.

Next to me, Ginger was looking through the vent.

"What does that sign say?" he asked, pointing a claw at a human pictogram.

I squinted at the human figures inside a box. "Not sure. A litter box?"

"Humans don't use litter boxes," Ginger said, condescendingly.

"They don't use our kind of litter boxes," I responded defensively, "but they litter inside a room that looks like a box." Connor was still being trained by his parents to litter in that room, so I often kept him company in there, encouraging him and distracting him.

Trip was snoring quietly now, so Ginger whispered his response. "We have to get out of here."

I wasn't sure what we should do. We had arrived at the hospital, but Connor was nowhere to be seen. This building had more floors than our house, so maybe he was on a different floor.

"What about that?" I asked, pointing at another human pictogram, this one with right angles stacked over each other. "That could mean stairs."

Ginger nodded slowly. "But how do we get down there? And through the door?"

I pawed at the vent underneath me, but it was Trip who answered.

"Those little screws in the corner of the vent cover, I bet between your claws and my paws we could get rid of them."

It took some work, but we came up with a process where I would wedge my claw into the metal screw and turn until the edge of the head peeked up. Then Trip would take over and turn the screw until it was all the way out with his fingers. He said that the screws were holding the vent cover in place. We did two screws and scared ourselves when the vent cover suddenly dropped open.

We sat there, claws out, ears on alert, waiting for a zombie to notice the noise, but none of them did.

I poked my head down through the hole in the ceiling, amazed that we hadn't been discovered. A look down the hallway answered my question. The zombies were gathered around some unfortunate mammal, eating it. I wondered if it was alive when they caught it. Despite my predator nature, I hoped it wasn't.

Ginger's orange head poked down next to mine, "They're busy; we should go!"

I silently agreed, though this vent felt way safer than the laminate floor below us. "Trip, wait here until we get the door open," Ginger said and leapt down the ten feet to the grimy tiled floor. The zombies didn't move, so when Ginger looked up at me, I swallowed my fear like a too-large piece of kibble and jumped, landing soundlessly beside him. We carefully edged our way to the door beside the stair pictogram.

On my hind paws, I walked my front paws up to the metal bar and put my weight on it, pushing. It moved infinitesimally forward. Ginger mimicked my stance and I felt it give way.

"Now, Trip!" Ginger hissed, falling to all fours and scooting into the stairwell. I streaked in behind him and we both stared up at the raccoon head poking down through the vent.

"Ok!" he said as the door started to close behind us. "On the count of three. One ...."

"Hurry!" Ginger yelled, giving up on stealth.

"Two ...."

My paws scrabbled for purchase on the smooth door. "Trip!" I wailed as the door slid shut with a whooshing sound.

We called and called through the closed door but couldn't hear anything on the other side. No squeals of terror from our friend nor shambling sounds from the zombies. The door handle on this side required thumbs, which was frustratingly ironic because of the raccoon on the other side who was the only one (zombies included) who could open it.

We scratched at the door, yowled our frustration, and eventually slunk away to the stairs. Ginger angrily wiped away his tears as we descended to the floor below. My reaction was worse: I was hoarse from calling for Trip and sick to my stomach with guilt. I kept hiccupping away tears, annoying Ginger to no end. I had told Trip he could go back to that comfortable apartment when we found Connor. I knew that even when I found Connor I would still feel terrible about losing Trip.

The door on the floor below was the same design as the one between us and Trip and I began to fear that we had traded one prison for another.

Another two floors and we were getting desperate when Ginger stopped suddenly, his ears cocking to the side. I listened too and realized I could hear voices.

"Humans," I said, my despair falling away like winter fur in the spring.

We raced down the flight of stairs to see a door wedged open with a bucket. I leapt over it and into the hallway, looking everywhere for the source of the voices.

"Pickles! Wait!" I could hear Ginger calling, but I was in a frenzy. Connor was close! I could almost scent him!

I careened around a corner and into a large room filled with couches, stopping short. Ginger caught up to me and we stood there, shoulder to shoulder looking at the two humans sitting in front of us. They looked terrible and smelled worse, hovering somewhere between alive and dead.

They sat on either side of a door holding large weapons and talking quietly between coughs and wheezes. Human backpacks, clothing, and toys were strewn here and there all around them.

One noticed us and raised his weapon our way, but his partner put a hand on his shoulder. "They're harmless, Eli. Leave 'em be."

"You sure?" The one named Eli coughed doubtfully.

"What could they do to us worse than these bites?" the partner said, pointing to a chunk of flesh missing in her leg.

Ginger and I backed up: they were bitten.

"See, they're smart enough to understand we're dead anyway," she said, nodding at us. "Keep running, kitties. Nothin' here but the soon-to-be dead."

"Pickles, let's go," Ginger said.

But my eyes were on the pile of human toys. I slowly sniffed towards them. Something in here was familiar. I took a look at the wounded humans and decided it was worth the risk. I stuck my head in the pile and pulled out a stuffed horse, backing up with it between my teeth until I was beside Ginger again.

"Pickles, what in the Saber has gotten into you?"

"This is Connor's," I declared, allowing my pet's scent to wash over me. "He's had it since I was a kitten."

Ginger knew better than to ask if I was sure. "Then he was here."

"Yes," I agreed, wishing I could carry this to my pet. He must be so upset to have left it behind. I looked around; where could he be? What would compel him to drop his stuffed horse like this? Who are these humans? Do they know Connor?

Ginger was looking at the door between the humans. "They're guarding this door. Like lions at the entrance to a cave."

I cocked my head, confused. Why would they be guarding the door? Where did the door lead? "They were bitten, so they were left behind?"

"Or they stayed behind and got bitten for their noble act," Ginger answered. "It doesn't matter. What matters is that your pet, and perhaps mine, are down that path."

I pawed at the stuffed horse thoughtfully. "What do we do?"

"We go back to Wally, like we said we would," Ginger said.

"Yeah," I replied, the idea of home so powerful I could almost smell my favorite pillow, and Connor's ratty old blankie. But thinking about Connor made me look through the doorway again. If he was just through the open door, shouldn't I keep going?

DAY THIRTEEN

Ginger and I sat on the topmost shelf of a laundry closet, directly facing the open door and the dying humans guarding it. We had decided to get some rest, and then make our way back home. Actually, Ginger had decided that. I was still on the fence. The darkness of that doorway was calling me. Telling me Connor was still within reach.

The humans lost interest in us as their deterioration continued, but we learned a lot about the zombie condition by observing and listening to them. There was a radio broadcast advising all surviving humans to unite at their local hospitals, which for Connor and his parents, was this location. Eli and Bree spent a lot of their night speculating about family members, making excuses for why they weren't here already. I'd watched enough horror movies from under the couch to think that maybe they weren't coming. My own small spark of hope was kept alive by that stuffed horse. I knew Connor had made it this far at least. But what should I do now?

The humans were attacked by a shuffling zombie wearing a white mask late at night and they dispatched it by hacking at its head. I hid under a large towel and backed so far into the laundry shelf that my tail hit the back of the closet, Ginger right beside me. I could still see the fight though, and as terrifying as it was, I learned something. Despite the chaotic way the humans fought and their ill-advised screams of anger, it seemed a more effective attack than the one I witnessed from my window seat last week, because this zombie stayed down. We waited hours for it to rise again, and when it did not, we talked about the significance of dealing a blow to the head.

The female human was in the last stages of her death, barely able to drag herself back to the doorway after the battle. Eli did his best to help her, but he was not much better.

"Ginger," I said coming to a decision and waking the orange cat up.

"I want to keep going," I said, massaging my towel

between my paws. "I want to look for Connor through that door."

"Are you kidding me?" Ginger answered, his eyes snapping open wide.

"We don't have to go far, but I know if I go back now, I'm going to spend the whole walk home wondering if Connor is just through that door," I said, the words coming out in a nervous jumble. I took a deep breath before I continued. "I have to know. I'm really scared, and I totally get it if you can't come with me, but I have to know."

"That's crazy," Ginger said, shaking his head at me. "You can't just go off on your own. Connor might not even be down there."

"Or he might be. With your pet. And Wally's pets," I replied. "I have to know."

The humans, meanwhile, had settled in to discussing how they would seal the doors against their eventual transformation into zombies.

"No one else is coming, Bree," Eli gasped, pulling a couch in the direction of the doorway,

"We're locking them in the sewers," she replied, trying to catch her breath.

"That's what we all agreed to," he grunted. "To hold this position until no one else showed up and then close it behind them."

"We don't need to do much," Bree half sobbed.

"Once we're zombies we won't remember how to use doorknobs."

Eli kept pushing the couch. "Might as well be sure."

I stood up. "I'm going, Ginger."

When he made no move to stop me, I realized I had to make a move: follow through with this plan or tuck my tail between my legs and follow him home. I remembered how Ginger had leapt onto Cinnamon's rooftop and waited for me to take my first step. I could do this. I had to do this.

I leapt down from our safe haven and brazenly walked towards the doorway, not even trying to disguise my destination. If the humans tried to stop me, I was going to bolt through their legs and make for the door.

Eli huffed, arming sweat off his brow. "Turns out we have two last customers."

I looked behind me to see Ginger had leapt down too and was following my lead. I smiled at him, feeling better and worse about this plan. Better because I wouldn't be alone. Worse because last time I had convinced a mammal to come with me, we lost him in the ceilings of the hospital a few floors up. I meowed up at the man named Eli, explaining our mandate.

"No way he understood that," Ginger said through his teeth.

"Do you think they're following a scent?" Bree asked, sliding to the floor beside the door. Eli didn't answer —

he was using all his energy to move the couch — but as I passed Bree, I purred up at her.

She smiled — understanding, I believe — and closed her eyes for the last time as a human. Then we were on the other side, standing on a darkened staircase. I looked back to see Eli closing the door behind us, the couch finalizing the act with a definitive thud.

It turns out that through that doorway were steps that led down to something humans call sewers. Ginger was happy to explain the use of sewers in the human litter process, and yes, they are as disgusting as you think they are. Like the streets and buildings above, humans had created maze-like designs below the earth. Sewers are a special kind of hell for a cat. Not only are they filled with our two worst enemies — rats and water — but they smell like wet dog and cucumbers. Numbers three and five on the worst list. Don't ask what number four is.

"I don't know how much longer I can stand this," Ginger said, stepping carefully around what we could only hope was a sodden pile of leaves. It was fortunate that we had rested in the comfort of clean towels, because neither of us would close our eyes down here.

"Just a few more minutes," I replied through chattering teeth, glancing at the ladder and manhole cover just ahead of us. We could see the pale sunlight drifting down to us through the holes in the iron covers that punctuated our subterranean journey. Surely we could escape this situation through them. I had to hope that we would find Connor soon.

Ginger sniffed, and I wondered how many more manholes we would pass before he took me up on my suggestion and left me alone to this hell. I couldn't blame him. He had never felt about his pets the way I felt about Connor. Actually, I don't think Ginger felt this way for anyone but himself.

"Have you sniffed anything from your pet?" he asked.

"Not since the stuffed horse," I admitted, allowing sarcasm to sharpen my tone, "though it's hard to discern any one smell down here. They're all so lovely."

"Didja hear that, Harold?" said a voice that made us jump. "She sounds like she's insulting our hospitality!"

I couldn't see where the voice came from, it echoed all around us. Ginger jumped up and onto the ladder, raising himself up, so I followed, sitting tensely on a rung directly below him. My fur was damp but still managed to stand on end in reaction to that spooky voice coming out of the darkness.

"Who are you?" he called out.

"Who are we?" replied the voice, sounding like many voices. "What a riddle!"

"What riddle?" I replied, my hackles so far up my back that I must have look like I'd been electrocuted.

"Capital idea, a riddle before you pass," the voice continued with a cackle. Ginger took another rung up, so I followed. This was bad juju. And that was saying something considering the zombies, insulting eagles, and dying humans we had just passed through.

"Here's one: what can you swallow, but also swallows you?" the voice said, and then shushed its own echo. Creepy much?

We kept moving up the rungs of the ladder, hoping to outrun the voice. "Uh ... not sure," I said, my teeth chattering so hard I don't think I could have formed complex words. "Any idea, Ginger?"

"Darkness?" Ginger tried, only a few rungs from the manhole cover now. What we were going to do at the top, I had no idea. There was no way two cats could lift a manhole cover, but that was the next problem.

"We'll give you a hint," the voice cackled at us from below. "Harold? A hint for our guests!"

Too late, I realized there were eyes all around us in this tunnel. They leapt as one, hundreds of rats dragging us into the watery answer below.

I WOKE SHIVERING and soaking wet in a cage.

"Water," I spat out. "That's the answer to your stupid riddle!"

"Thank the Saber, I thought they'd drowned you," said Ginger from his own cage.

I shook myself, spraying water and who-knew-what-else at Ginger, who cringed.

"Sorry," I said, glad Wally wasn't with us. He would have sent me to the stocks for that. I took a better look at our situation. We were in two cages, the kind humans would use to keep a bird, suspended from the ceiling of the sewer, winched up with ropes. This was so much worse than the stocks. I pushed at the bars of the cage. Except for the small cat carriers our pets used to transport us to the vet, I'd never been in such an enclosed space. I hated it. I hated everything about this situation. The water, the cages, but especially that creepy voice.

"How did rats raise us up here?" I asked, astonished.

"Oh, we helped Harold out," said that disembodied voice out of the darkness below.

Many voices chuckled at us and I saw the beady eyes of the rats staring up at us raptly.

"What do you want?" Ginger asked, his voice shaking slightly, though from the damp or fear, I could not tell.

A ghostly white figure stole out of the shadows below. "Want? We have what we want! Entertainment for Harold!"

"Who is Harold?" I asked the speaker, trying to get a better look at the animal. It was either a huge albino rat or some kind of opossum. Either way, I was creeped out. Have you ever read a book where an opossum was a good guy? Yeah, me neither.

The animal snickered, waving its pink paws all around.

"This is Harold," he said. "Naming each of them was tiresome, so they are all Harold."

A splashing sound was followed by a groan I recognized all too well. From the recess of one of the walls, a zombie strained against his bonds. I froze in my cage. This was their entertainment? The zombie was wearing a long, white coat and something around its neck was holding it fast, not allowing it to move any closer to us. It stretched its arms towards us and gnashed its teeth though, clear about what it *wanted* to do.

"What kind of monsters are you?" I whispered, looking down at the white devil who was giggling fit to burst. "Let us go!"

"So demanding!" the opossum declared, clapping its paws. "Perhaps you will be more entertaining than our last few visitors."

He pointed at his feet where the bones of small mammals could be seen. "The humans took the last trains south. No one left to sport with but this fellow."

"We have to get out of here," I said, turning to look at Ginger, hoping he had a brilliant escape plan. But Ginger was cowering in his cage, sobbing big gulping tears as he stared at the zombie reaching for him.

"Ginger!" I called, shocked at his response. "Ginger, it's okay! We're going to be okay!"

"Well, I don't know about that," the opossum corrected, pressing a paw to his chest dramatically. "I have a soft spot for filthy felines such as yourselves, but Harold does enjoy scaredy cats, it's true! Why, I remember that pernicious skunk we caught two nights ago ... Or was it three nights ...?"

I felt my cage moving up and looked around for the source of the motion. The rats were raptly listening to the opossum's monologue, but I was moving half an inch at a time towards the ceiling, away from the zombie, the rats, and the crazy supervillain leading them.

"Ginger," I called, trying to draw his eyes from the zombie, "focus on me instead." For some reason, Ginger's fear was giving me strength. I had to be the brave one. I owed him that.

He finally turned his face towards me, his whiskers shaking as he spoke. "I failed, Pickles."

His cage started moving up, as well, as I realized this was no random zombie. This was Ginger's pet. The one who worked at the hospital. My heart thudded dully for him. He did care for more than himself! His mission had failed. No wonder he was distraught. I would be a puddle of cat tears at the bottom of this cage if that were zombie-Connor tied to a wall.

"Hey! You! Let go of those cats!" the opossum shrieked, as my cage hit the ceiling of the sewer with a bang. Deft black paws pulled the locks apart and I looked up into a masked face I never thought to see again.

"Coming?" Trip said with a cheeky grin.

I was so surprised it took me a moment to leap up into the round pipe where he stood, pulling at Ginger's cage now. All around, rats scampered towards us, but now I was angry, and I felt Wally's instructions on self-defense take me over. Leaning out of the pipe, I swiped left and right, knocking them off the sewer walls and sending them screaming down into the hands of Ginger's once-pet.

The opossum was losing his mind down there, shrieking and cursing his falling army, but even when Trip pulled Ginger free and called me to follow, I kept up my attack on the rats; I was so angry at the way they had treated Ginger's pet. How many had they killed for their sport as the world fell around them?

I smacked a rat full in the face and she hit one of the cages hard enough to knock it free. It dropped with a loud crash and it must have connected with whatever was holding the zombie in place because, with a great surge, he broke free and grabbed the opossum with both hands. That was enough for me. I took a last swipe at the rat army and turned tail, running up the pipe after Trip and Ginger.

Trip led us up a drain pipe into something he called a "convenience store," popping the cover off with a triumphant grunt. As soon as I was through, we slid it back into place, and Trip pushed a heavy box of tinned vegetables over it. There was no way anyone was going to be able to follow us up that drain pipe.

We sat puffing with exhaustion for a moment and then I threw myself at the large raccoon.

"I'd scent you if I didn't stink so badly!" I said with a grin, wrapping my tail around him.

He gave a huge belly laugh. "Well, I know how you cats hate the water, but there is a sink over there, if you want to use it."

With Trip's help, we filled the sink with lukewarm water and sank into it despite our aversion to the liquid. Ginger just followed our directions without speaking. After a complete immersion, we sat him down on a heating vent, where I began licking the both of us clean as Trip filled us in on his story.

"Once that door closed, I was sure I was zombie food," Trip said, shaking his head as he dragged over a pile of snacks. He ripped open a small bag of cat food and pushed it my way. Since leaving the safety of my house, I'd discovered it was hard work finding something to eat that wasn't pre-packaged in a bag. Humans obviously stored food here for the cats, dogs, and hamsters in their lives, and as I looked around, I saw more variety and bounty than I had ever seen in the world outside. Animals like this raccoon had no such luxuries. No wonder Trip and his ilk picked through the rubbish bins behind human houses. And no wonder so many of them lived in the human-dense cities. What were we going to do once the humans didn't have time to make us these precious bags of kibble? I took a grateful mouthful of cat food, chewing over the problem, and I made Ginger take a bite as well.

"Did you jump down after it closed?" I asked, wishing for a drink of water. Trip seemed to anticipate my needs because he pointed to a bowl on the floor behind the counter. I smelled dog around the bowl, but ignored it; beggars can't be choosers, after all. This store really was convenient; the humans named it well.

"I did jump down, but as soon as I put my paws on the handle, two zombies came around the corner."

I shook my head. "And?"

"I guess I panicked," Trip admitted, his mouth full of jerky and chips. "I lapped the floor four times dodging zombies and calling for help."

"We couldn't get back through the door," I said apologetically, feeling the guilt swirl back up. "I swear we tried."

"I was in such a frenzy, I don't know if I would have noticed if you were my den mother holding a turkey dinner," Trip said, swallowing an enormous bite and looking at the bottom of the chip bag as if surprised he had reached the end. I snagged another from the shelf and brought it down to him.

"And then I tripped over something as I was trying to get away from a zombie and slid into the open elevator shaft," he explained in a voice that said this kind of thing had happened before.

"Holy cats!"

"Yeah, it was not the best route down to the sewers, but it was direct!" he said as he ripped open the new bag of chips.

"How did you survive the fall?" Ginger asked.

Trip shrugged. "I grabbed at these ropes hanging in the center, and the zombies didn't follow. Then I climbed down, all the way to the bottom floor. The elevator was there so I couldn't actually get out on the floor, but the pipes in the ceiling were open, so I took them instead, thinking they might lead out to the street."

I licked crumbs off my face, glad Ginger was speaking again. "And you found this store?"

"After hours and hours of wandering, I smelled it, yes. Made it all the way under the drain we just came through when I heard your voice, Pickles."

"And you came back for us?" Ginger asked, regarding the raccoon with a new respect.

"Of course I did. I gave you my oath," Trip said. "Followed your voice down to where I found you. Saw the cages and how they were tied to the ceiling and started pulling you up."

"Trip, you saved our lives," I said, standing up and scenting the raccoon. "Thank you."

Trip actually looked a little embarrassed at the praise,

pulling at his black whiskers.

"That opossum said the humans took the last train south," I said. "What did he mean? What is a train?"

Ginger's ears came up. "What do you mean? You can't mean to go on!"

"There are train tracks behind this building," Trip answered, earning a glare from Ginger and a grin from me. "You could follow them south. A train is something I usually avoid because it's huge, fast, and carries a lot of humans and not much food, though I guess those days are gone. The humans are in hiding, but their tunnels remain. Weird. Anyways, Pickles, trains are basically like a really long car that can't turn except on the tracks."

"There you have it," I said, trying to imagine this vehicle and failing. "Connor and his parents took that … train. I will find them and bring them home.

"Trip, this is the safest you've been since meeting us. I can't ask you to keep risking your life," I said, pacing around in front of them. "And Ginger, you have suffered a terrible blow. No one would blame you for going home and regrouping."

Ginger shook his whiskers. "Pickles, it's time to go home. We've done everything we can."

"That's not true. I haven't found Connor. But if you could report back to Wally on my progress," I said, giving him a new mission, "that would be a great help to me."

DAY FIFTEEN

Saying goodbye to my friends was incredibly hard, but I knew Ginger's heart was broken, and I worried that his distraction could get him killed. He promised to report everything back to Wally and do his best to help him.

Trip drew a map in the dirt to show me how to keep heading south, but as Ginger and I explained, cats always know which way to go. It's like landing on our feet even when we jump from a very high spot. Cats have perfect directional sense. But I did take a moment to ask Trip to watch out for Ginger until I got back.

We set out at the same time, me towards the railway tracks and them back towards home, above ground along the streets as long as they could.

I watched them until they were out of sight, skirting between vehicles. I wished them the very best. I also sent up a silent prayer to the Saber that Trip would not get them killed. Really, with those two, it could go either way.

Part of me wanted to follow them so badly that I had to sit down to stop my knees from shaking. I had never been on my own before. Not completely alone. Not like this. I'd lost Connor's scent from the horse stuffy, the plunge into the sewer waters denying me even that. But if I concentrated, I could see his broad smile, feel his pudgy fingers, hear the sound of his heartbeat as he slept beside me.

In front of me was a long road of tracks, but at least I would be able to see aggressors from far away. I set out, walking between the tracks. Trip said that if that really was the last train, I would be safe, but if I felt any vibration along the metal I was to get off the tracks like a coyote was chasing me. The midday sun had risen over my left shoulder, so I knew I was traveling south, hopefully to find Connor and the rest of the humans who had escaped the zombies.

I spent my first night alone in pouring rain, shivering under a bridge. Rain is horrible, and much worse than the warm baths Wally's pets sometimes subjected us to. I don't think I slept more than a half hour for worry I would wake to the growling sounds of a zombie pack.

I argued with myself all night about giving up and going home or continuing on this mission to find Connor. Somehow, the mission won out. But only by a little, and probably because I dreamed of Connor's smiling face.

The second day I witnessed a Shih-Tzu being chased by some slow-moving zombies. I tipped over a metal garbage can to distract the pack of zombies, and then ungracefully scrambled up on top of a car, dropping low so no one (alive or dead) could see me. I was too scared to move for an hour, but I was glad to see the dog escape.

But it was on the fifth day of my lonely trek that my life changed forever.

DAY TWENTY

"Now, what do we have here?"

A silken voice woke me from a nightmare of teeth and water.

"No more riddles," I mumbled as I staggered to my feet. I had finally allowed myself to fall asleep in an abandoned car beside the tracks. The back window had been rolled down far enough for me to squeeze through, and I had gorged myself on the cold fries in the backseat before passing out. Other than garbage, what did animals outside the house eat on a daily basis?

I turned around in a circle on the backseat, not seeing the source of the voice, and suddenly terrified it was that evil white opossum again, haunting my every step.

"Up here," called the voice, and my eyes swung up to the sun roof, where the most beautiful creature I had ever seen sat licking her paws. She was an Abyssinian, a breed I had read about in *One Hundred and One Dalmatians*. I knew her coat was ticked with shades of gold and that her eyes were like burnished copper. I tried to speak, and found I had to swallow to make my voice engage.

"I ... How ... Hello," I finally managed, wondering if the sun followed her around to make sure she glowed everywhere she went.

"Hello," she replied with a toothy grin. "You on your own, little lady?"

The question flipped my paranoid switch and I jumped onto the back window well to take a better look around us. "I might be, I might not. How about you ... little lady?"

If possible, her grin got even wider at my throwing the term back at her. She was not little, she was long and lithe in a way my breed would never be.

"I tend to rub other mammals the wrong way," she replied, not really answering the question. "You done with those fries?"

I looked down at the leftovers and decided they were fair game. "All yours."

She slid down the side of the car and through the same open window I had used. I gave her space, staying on higher ground just in case, like Wally had always told me, but she moved without fear, eating the fries slowly, obviously not as ravenous as I had been the night before.

"There's more than enough to share," she said, looking up at me with those liquid eyes.

I considered denying my hunger, but my stomach growled loudly in direct opposition. She laughed, a deep sound that was both unsettling and enticing at the same time. I was becoming as stupid as a mouse in her presence. Defiantly, I jumped down to her side and took a bite of cold fries.

"My name is Hannah," she said, pausing between bites.

"Pickles," I answered.

"The salty lumps sealed in jars of vinegar?" she asked with another deep laugh. I stuck my head back into the fries so she wouldn't see my embarrassment.

"Your pet must have been in an ironic mood to name such a beautiful cat after such an odd thing."

I would have smiled at the compliment if not for the reminder of my pet, and how this graceful distraction had made me forget him for a moment.

"I should probably go," I said, cleaning the salt from my whiskers.

I jumped up to the armrest, looking over my shoulder, sure I would never see such a glorious feline ever again. "Good luck, Hannah."

"Wait, where are you going?" she called.

"I'm on a mission to find my pet," I explained, and

pushed myself through the window. I landed on the ground and started walking towards the tracks to resume my journey. I had only gone about ten yards when she caught up to me.

"Surely all missions were canceled when the zombies appeared? The circle of life is in flux. We must adapt," she said, falling into step beside me.

"My pet is only two in human years," I said, "and I've received no word of his safety or the end of the mission."

She absorbed that, and then said, "How can you even be sure he's alive if he is a youngling?"

I explained finding Connor's stuffed horse at the hospital as we reached the tracks. I made sure the sun was in the east, and that I was still headed south, and kept walking. Train cars littered our path for several miles, some on the tracks, some tipped on their sides. I checked each one for humans, but they all seemed to be empty.

When she made no move to withdraw or turn away, I had to ask, "Where are your pets?"

"I told you," she answered, shaking her head. "I don't get along with other mammals."

"You were never assigned a pet?" I asked, finding that hard to believe. Surely a cat that looked like her would be coveted among humans. They were notoriously shallow and picked their cats based on looks rather than skills. Though I supposed that when I was a kitten my best skill was my focused concentration on a moving piece of yarn. Really not much of a resume.

She didn't answer, stopping suddenly, her large pointed ears cocking to the side. I mimicked her and heard the light footsteps of other cats.

"Hide," she hissed and then she was gone, a flash of gold under the nearest train car. I had dropped low to follow her when two short-haired cats leapt into my path.

"We found you just in time. Didn't we, Liona?" said one to the other.

"Oh, indubitably, Jaguar, we did."

I stopped in my tracks, my heart hammering, trying not to look like I was looking for an escape route, but really, really looking for an escape route. "Your names are Jaguar and Liona?" I asked.

"Our slave names were moronic, so we adopted new ones when our pets turned," said Jaguar, sliding up close to me. "And what's your moniker my fine feline friend?"

I decided on the truth. "Pickles. Though I still have a pet, so I think I'll keep it."

Liona wrinkled her nose at the name. "Bast, we have to give this poor girl a new name."

A huge white cat waddled into our midst. "Agreed; we can't travel with a condiment."

All three cats laughed uproariously at that joke, and

I tried to demonstrate my lack of concern by licking at my whiskers. Really, I had no idea how to get out of this situation, and Hannah seemed freaked out, so I was officially on high alert. Then again, I'd faced zombies, eagles, and an army of rats led by a mad opossum. I was having a bit of a weird week.

Bast squinted her eyes at me. "Oh, this is a cool customer here."

"Look, I don't want any trouble," I admitted, amazed my fake relaxation technique was working and wondering if Hannah was still in earshot. "I really need to get going. And it's not safe to just be talking out here in the middle of nowhere."

"Ain't that the truth," Liona said, "which is why we're traveling as a pack."

I nodded: that made sense. "Where are you headed?"

"The highlands, where humans are rare and fowl and rodent are plentiful," Bast said, nodding her head westwards. I guess that answered my question as to what cats ate when they were outside the house. Gross.

"Bast had a vision, she did," Liona explained reverently, "the first night the dead humans rose. She was touched by the Saber."

I suspected that all three of these cats were touched by something. And it rhymed with crazy.

"You can come with us," Jaguar said. "Every claw is a help."

"Well, almost every claw," Bast interjected, throwing a meaningful glance at her followers.

"Thanks for the offer, but the thing is, I'm following the trail of my pet. He's a youngling and he needs my help." I rose, starting to walk away, and hoping for the best. The "best" being that they walk in the opposite direction.

The cats looked at each other. "A noble quest," said Bast, licking her lips nervously, "but I must insist."

I felt my heart rate accelerate again, and a bit of that anger rose in my throat. "Insist all you want, but unless you have proof that Connor is in these highlands you speak of, I'm heading south."

"If you're not with us," Bast said, arching her back, "you're against us."

I hissed in response, all my anger at zombies and missing pets exploding to the surface. "This is ridiculous! You can't force every cat you come across to follow you!"

"You will respect Bast's vision!" screeched Liona, and she vaulted at me. I leapt straight up, swiping with my left paw in mid-air and landing on the other side of the tracks. I think I was more surprised than she was when I actually connected with her leg. She yowled in pain, but I took too long staring at my success because by the time I turned to run, Jaguar threw himself at me. I was sure I was a goner, but a blur of gold came flying at him from under a train car. I used his confusion to scoop dust into the black cat's eyes with my paw before rolling underneath him and swiping at his tender belly. He collapsed into a defensive ball at my paws.

Bast was no fighter, she fled screaming, calling for Liona and Jaguar to save her.

I huffed, hissing and twice my usual size as the other two cats dragged themselves after their pathetic prophet. Only when they were small dots on the landscape did I lower my arch.

"You're hurt!" exclaimed Hannah from somewhere out of my sight.

That's when the pain overtook my adrenaline rush and I fell to my side, unconscious.

DAY TWENTY-ONE

"Stay still!" Hannah said, her face blurry in front of my eyes.

I groaned, the pain flooding over me anew, I would have thrown up if I could muster the energy. I hated throwing up.

"Stop moving!"

"I can't help it," I mumbled. "What happened?"

"That alley cat, Liona, tried to gut you, that's what," Hannah spat out, pressing something cold against my belly. I managed to stifle a cry, taking short breaths until I felt like I might not die of pain.

"Where are we?" I asked finally.

"Inside one of the train cars," Hannah replied, sitting back on her haunches.

My eyes were starting to unblur, and I could see huge shapes moving in the darkness.

"Hannah," I cried out, alarmed.

She glanced over her shoulder. "Horses. They're harmless."

"Harmless?" I repeated doubtfully, running my eyes over the animals, their eyes were those of prey, but their sheer size made it hard to see them that way. Also, you may not know this, but large prey animals produce very large piles of litter. Like, cat-sized piles. Wally-sized-cat piles. We were surrounded by these piles.

"I figured Bast would be too scared to come after us in here," Hannah answered, as I tried very hard not to inhale, "and the horses haven't eaten their way through their food supply yet, so they seem docile ... for now."

I winced, lying back on my side with effort. "You got me in here? How?"

Hannah pointed at a grate in the floor. "I dragged you under the train car, but Helios pulled you through the grate."

"Helios?" I asked.

"Pleased to meet you, Pickles," nickered one of the huge mammals, a speckled specimen directly above us.

"I ... pleased to meet you as well, Helios," I managed to answer before fading out again.

DAY TWENTY-TWO

"Calm yourself, small cat," a deep voice said from the darkness.

"Hannah? Where is Hannah?"

"She went to replenish our water supply, small cat. Stop moving around or the webbing will tear."

"Webbing?" I slurred, looking down at my belly. Was that spider webbing? What in the Saber was happening to me?

DAY TWENTY-THREE

"The water is coming from a hose?" I asked, looking at the overflowing bucket near me.

"It was directing rain water away from the roof; I simply redirected it in here," Hannah replied, checking my webbing. "Your belly wound has scabbed over. How are you feeling?"

"Alive," I answered gratefully, sitting up to scoop water into my mouth, "thanks to you."

She gave me a sad smile. "I'm the reason you're wounded at all."

"What do you mean? I'm the one who didn't move fast enough when you told me to hide," I answered, taking a tentative bite of the food she had brought. It was a very old piece of hamburger, and it tasted like an old shoe, but I forced myself to swallow it, nonetheless. I had to regain my strength. I'd lost days to those fanatical felines, and I needed to get back on the road to Connor.

Hannah batted a piece of hay before answering. "Bast called me a curse," she explained in a quiet voice, "and she was right to. Everyone around me has died, from my mother and siblings to my first pet to those terrible cats who attacked you."

I stayed silent, allowing her to continue, sensing she needed to get this out.

"There were six of them before, you know," Hannah said. "Bast, Liona, Jaguar, el Gato, Solomon, and Tiger."

I would have laughed out loud at the ridiculous renaming strategy of these cats, but, looking at Hannah's down-turned mouth, I restrained myself. She had been abused and rejected and I didn't need to add to that pain. Quite the opposite. "What happened to the last three?" I asked instead.

"I was the last to join, and I did so willingly," Hannah answered. "I was tired of staying awake to dodge the zombies, and though I didn't buy the idea of a dream land, I had no direction in mind. I was basically just surviving. So, west seemed like as good a direction as any. The very first night, I took watch with Solomon," Hannah said, "and while we were comparing our first notice of the zombies, we were attacked by a pack of dogs."

I was horrified, but unsurprised. When the natural order is upended, you could rely on animals, even domesticated ones, to return to their base instincts.

"They didn't actually intend to eat us I don't think," Hannah said. "I tried to talk to them, to make them see reason, but Bast had a better plan. She offered me, promising no fight, no struggle, if the rest of the cats could leave unmolested."

I wished that fat white cat was sitting in front of me with her smug smile so that I could smack it right off her face. With a horseshoe. Instead, I rubbed my face against Hannah's, trying to console her.

"At first, the dogs seemed to agree, and Bast actually tried to convince me to go along with it!" Hannah said, regaining some of the fire I had seen the first day we met as she described the scene. "She said it was all part of her grand dream, that songs would be sung of my sacrifice when they reached the promised land."

"She really was cat-nipped crazy," I said with a low growl.

Hannah nodded, losing some of her smile. "But when I refused to just fall into their paws, one of the dogs, a whippet I think, he … moved so fast. One minute, I was standing next to Tiger, the next she was gone, dragged into the bushes, crying for help."

I shook my head in disgust.

"It was a blur after that," Hannah said with a gulp of water. "Every cat for themselves. I don't know how I got away, but I could hear Bast screaming at me at the top of her voice for a very long time. Calling me a curse."

Helios leaned down and nuzzled the top of Hannah's head. His nostril was the size of my torso, but I managed not to flinch away.

"You have shown us nothing but loyalty and aid, Hannah of the Felines," he said in his deep voice. "You must forget the words of that ignoble beast."

The rest of the horses in the train car nodded their agreement, and I looked to Hannah, hoping she would take heart from their support, but she had eyes only for me. I bowed my head in agreement. "Hannah, I would be honored to journey with you. You called yourself a curse, but you saved me. I would have died at the paws of those cats if you hadn't leapt in. Or afterwards, if you hadn't surrounded me with these huge animals and covered me in spider bandages. You're the opposite of a curse. You're a gift."

She laughed at that, a sound that was a better balm than any food or treatment administered to me since I was wounded.

DAY TWENTY-FIVE

"Are you sure you can do it without hurting yourself?" Hannah asked me for the third time.

I wasn't sure, but I nodded anyway, pushing up on the metal rod with my head, ignoring its weight and the rusty sound it made as it fought against the ring that held it.

This was the key and lock holding the horses in this train car, and before I could continue on my quest, we had to help them escape their prison. They had, after all, kept me safe while I recovered. I knew nothing of horses before meeting this small group, but they seemed to me to be a fine group of mammals, with a nobility I had never encountered before.

"Is it even moving?" I grunted at Helios, who from this vantage point on the outside of the train car, I could see through a thin slit in the door.

"It moves, yes, Pickles," he replied. "Keep pushing."

I did, pressing up until I felt like the metal rod was drilling into the top of my head. A bit more of this and you would be able to hang me from a Christmas tree like an ornament, complete with my own hook through the head.

"It has stopped moving up," Helios said. "Release it, young feline, before you damage yourself again."

I would have shaken my head, but that would drop the rod. I felt Hannah winding herself around me and nearly dropped it out of surprise.

"Let me try," she said, putting her head under my chin and pushing up as well.

"Mm mph!" I cried, tears falling as my poor skull was bruised.

"Stop!" Helios begged, and we let the rod drop with a sigh of relief. (Okay, mine might have been a cry of relief.)

"Ow," I muttered, rubbing a paw on the top of my head.

Hannah bounded on top of the train car to look down at the rod from above.

"If I could pull it from here as you push it from below," she speculated, "we might manage it."

She wrapped her teeth around the metal and gave me a small nod. I dutifully pushed up again with my bruised head, but we got no further than before.

"Enough, feline heroes," Helios said after our third attempt. "A valiant effort, but it would seem our fates are out of your paws."

I joined Hannah on the roof, hanging my head down over the side to talk to Helios. "We'll think of something else."

"You have delayed your quest too long as it is," answered Helios, echoing my heart's fear. "When you find your pets, perhaps you will convince them to come back here and free us."

"They'll be long dead by then," whispered Hannah, her tail twitching as she stalked back and forth on the roof, "and that's if we manage to communicate with your humans. In my experience they are terrible linguists. My pet never understood a thing I said."

"Connor is only two, so he can still understand most of what I say to him," I said. "Wally said he'll lose that ability as he gets older." The thought made my heart hurt a little — to know that the understanding Connor and I had had since we were younglings was fading as he got older, but that was the way of life. The younger a human is, the closer to nature and other animals they are.

Hannah tilted her head. "But how good is Connor at communicating with the older pets?"

"Shh …," I replied, dropping down into a flat crouch. I heard mammals approaching. Hannah flattened beside me and Helios hushed his peers inside the train car. Seconds passed and we heard the groans of zombies, as they dragged themselves our way.

I turned wide eyes towards Hannah, and she returned the stare, her whiskers twitching a message of panic. I sent matching signals back. I didn't know what we should do, or where we could hide. Would we be safer inside the train car?

They slouched and groaned their way towards us, a group of four, of varying ages and stages of decay. I still had no idea what attracted them, was it smell? Sound? Jazz music? As predators went, zombies seemed to function under very different parameters. Whatever it was that drove them, the train car called their attention and they turned towards it, glazed eyes locked on it.

"What do we do?" Hannah's whiskers communicated.

"No idea," I tried to communicate back. Out of our many methods of communication between cats, the whiskers were the third most effective, followed only by the twitching of the tail, which was really only useful in communicating mood.

The zombies slammed against the train car with more violence than I expected from such slow-moving beasts. I cried out in alarm, drawing their attention our way, but not enough to stop their assault. They glanced up at us but groaned at the train car, shoving, pushing, and grunting. Despite the fact that they had no organization or communication between them, the smell of the horses within seemed to be enough to compel them to continue their efforts, and we could feel the train car starting to tip.

The horses panicked, though I could hear Helios trying to calm them, and Hannah called down to them as well. "If they knock the car on its side, the door may come loose! If it does, be ready to bolt."

"Run east to that tree on the rise," Helios commanded, trying to raise his voice above the stomping and neighing within and the battering sounds on the outside.

"What about us?" I yelled, now holding on to the train car's roof for dear life.

"When we tip, the zombies will swarm," Hannah yelled as I slid past her as the roof tipped beyond forty-five degrees. I managed to grab on to an edge with five claws. "If the door stays closed, we bolt to the tree, as Helios said."

"And if the door opens?" I yelled back.

"I don't know," she replied, her tail twitching with alarm.

"Then we distract the zombies until the horses are free," I said, twitching my determination back at her, trying to communicate as much courage as I could into each flick of my tail. Not an easy task when you're holding on by one paw and terrified for your life.

Ten times, twenty, the zombies hit the train car again and again, the sounds of their bodies and bones beating against the metal, gruesome and unyielding. One of my claws broke off, and I gritted my teeth, feeling the train car reach the tipping point.

That's when a new sound reached my ears: a high-pitched squeal coming at us from ground-level. I had a moment to wonder what new fresh hell this could be and then we were airborne. The train car finally released the tracks it had been sitting on, and with a deafening metallic crash, slammed onto its side.

Hannah and I sprang free seconds before the train car made contact with the ground. As we'd hoped, the door fell open with a noisy clang, but the horses inside were a jumble of long legs and terror.

The zombies hadn't noticed the open door yet. They were distracted by a small blur of brown that was weaving between their legs, screeching at the top of its lungs. I got my head in the doorway of the train car, calling for Helios, but it was mayhem, and I narrowly missed being kicked in the head by a frantic horse.

"Pickles!" yelled Hannah, pulling my attention out of the train car.

I expected to see her fending off a zombie, but instead, she was pointing at three new animals who had joined the fray. Except they weren't at all new to me.

"We're back!" announced Trip, a rope under his arm as he streaked past me. The other end of the rope was in the mouth of Ginger, who gave me a wink and then made a quick turn in the opposite direction. I saw what they were up to immediately — wrapping a long rope around three of the slow-moving humans — but the zombies were totally at a loss, their concentration on a tiny hamster who was still screeching at near supersonic sound levels. Ginger and Trip whipped around the zombies, but it was Wally who was calling out directions a few yards away.

"Left, Emmy!" he yelled. "No! Your other left, you daft hamster!"

I had never seen a hamster before and stood there with my mouth hanging open at this tiny furball of ferocity.

"Pickles," Helios roared, and I turned to see the fourth zombie had him by the leg, and was pulling him out of the train car, teeth gnashing in anticipation.

I noticed that its neck bone was almost entirely exposed, the flesh around it missing from bites and decomposition, and I remembered Eli and Bree's effective fight with the zombies. Removing the head was key.

"Helios, kick it in the head as hard as you can," I said, burrowing between horse bodies to get close to his ears.

"What?"

"The head," I repeated, as I was shoved right into Helios's forehead by horses struggling to get upright. "You have to knock its head right off its body. Can you do that?"

Instead of answering, Helios took a good look at the zombie pulling at his right leg and kicked it full in the face with his left leg. The head went sailing out of sight. I sat down on my haunches, shocked, but Helios immediately turned to organizing the other horses. Hannah looked through the long horse legs as they exited the train car, leaving just me and lots and lots of horse poop.

"I can't believe that worked," Hannah called from outside the train car.

"Me either," I replied honestly, trying to get up and failing. My legs were all wobbly.

"Better get out of here before the smell hits you," Hannah suggested.

I tried again and found that I could manage it, escaping the train car to see that Helios had led his horses over to the zombies Ginger and Trip had, well, tripped, for lack of a better word, and they were handily stomping those threats into dust. Unbound from the train car, the horses seemed to be quite handy at dealing with zombies.

"Well, aren't you going to say hello?" Wally asked, standing over me with a grin as wide as his girth.

What followed was the happiest reunion I have ever been a part of. With Hannah snuggled into my side, purring contentedly, each of us retold our stories, catching the group up as Helios and his troop went in search of fresh food and water.

We sat atop a train car a few yards away from the still bodies of the zombies. This one was still on the tracks and afforded us the added safety of height.

Emmy the hamster was the only one who couldn't seem to sit still, and scampered all around us, growling and squealing at the darkness, as if daring it to come at us.

"We made quick time back to the neighborhood," Ginger explained, "but we smelled it burning from far away."

I turned shocked eyes Wally's way, and he hung his head. "I was unable to save the home of our pets, despite turning on all the taps in the house."

The only fire I had ever seen was the one our pets lit in our little backyard in the summertime in a small metal container. They would roast something called a marshmallow over the heat at the end of a long stick. I would watch the white fluffy marshmallow catch the fire and turn black and then I would smell the acrid scent of burning sugar, not understanding why Connor would put it in his mouth. I tried to imagine what it would look like covering our little house and found I couldn't. Maybe that was a good thing.

"How did you get out?" Hannah asked.

"The cat door into the backyard," Wally said. "The one benefit of fire is that slow-moving zombies are both attracted to it and destroyed by it, so our neighborhood became a central location for the dead."

Trip burped loudly, and then apologized sheepishly. He had found a store of garbage in the train car we were sitting on and had just finished consuming it. None of us had been interested in the contents.

"Once I got outside, it was mayhem, with zombies flaming past me. They didn't care that they were being burned to ashes," Wally continued as Trip scuttled back into the train car to root for more supplies. "I climbed the oak tree out front of Cinnamon's house, directed some stunned squirrels to abandon their precious nuts, and got as high as I could get. That's when I saw Ginger and Trip."

"He called down to us," Ginger said, taking up the thread, "but like Wally said, it was a dangerous game of dodge-the-flaming-zombie to get to him. I ended up climbing the tree in front of Vance's house instead, with the intention of meeting Wally in the middle, but that's when we saw Emmy."

We all turned to look at the hamster who continued to circle us. Emmy noticed and bared her tiny yellow teeth.

"She was inside her house, which was ablaze. We could see her through the open window, holding a lit branch in her mouth and lighting zombies on fire," Wally said, shaking his head with amazement at the memory.

Trip climbed back on the roof carrying a bottle of water and a bag of tiny hot dogs. He distributed the hot dogs among us, and even coaxed Emmy into taking a bite.

"She doesn't talk?" I asked, watching her tuck into the hot dogs.

"We think she used to, but she's been in shock since Vance and Ralph died," Wally replied. "That hasn't stopped her from killing more zombies than any mammal her size should be able to. She's more useful than a legion of trained dogs."

Trip reached out to stroke Emmy, but she jerked away and returned to her patrol, leaving behind her half-finished meal. I found myself wondering how two mastiffs dealt with having a dictator hamster in charge. Were all hamsters this ... impressive?

"So, then what happened?" Hannah prompted, in between licking her paws clean of the salty hot dog treats.

Trip spoke up then, sitting back on his large behind and washing his paws with some of the water. "Well, we had to get her out of there, so I rapped on the window until she saw me."

"I still don't think she would have come out if she hadn't noticed that baby chipmunk losing her grip," Ginger said.

"Emmy came flying out from under the open window, but she streaked right past me and leapt for the tree between Wally and Ginger," Trip said, his eyes on the hamster now. "She had that baby chipmunk in hand and back on her mother's back before I had even figured out what she was up to."

Emmy walked through our midst, oblivious to the admiring eyes following her wiggling butt. We weren't actually admiring her butt, she just wiggled hypnotically when she walked and .... Oh, never mind.

"It was pretty clear we had to get the heck out of the trees, because they were catching flames from the idiot zombies below," Wally said, "and with no home to protect, I made the command decision to join your quest, Pickles."

"And you two?" I asked Trip and Ginger.

"Are you kidding?" Trip asked, looking around. "You cats are my best friends ever!"

Ginger shrugged, the melancholy of losing his pet still apparent in his whiskers and tail. "Trip and Wally aren't exactly natural allies, so I thought I would come along and act as ambassador."

Wally snorted, but in a friendly way, and Trip burst out laughing, holding his large belly.

I smiled at them all, touched and bolstered by their presence. "Together we will find Connor. I know we will."

DAY TWENTY-SIX

We set out the next morning at dawn with the blessings of our equine friends. Helios was especially sad to see us go, and even offered to take us as far as he could down the railway tracks before returning to his group, but we had no idea how far that might be, so we turned him down.

Their plan was to make it into the hills as far away from human populations as they could, but they promised that if that plan did not work, they would follow the railway to us. We in turn promised to leave signs if we turned from this path.

"Wait," Hannah said as I turned to lead the way. "Pickles, are you sure you want me to come with you?"

"What a question," I said, bumping my forehead to hers. "We need you."

"But what about ...."

"Please don't bring up that crazy fat cat again," I said.

"But ...," she trailed off, running her eyes over the animals who waited for us a few steps away. "You trust these mammals?"

I cast my eyes over them. We probably made the strangest fellowship since the one in *The Lord of the Rings*, with a wizard, an elf, a dwarf, a bunch of hobbits, and some men. Those books had been some of my favorites, and I couldn't help but wonder how those travelers would have seen us: four cats and a raccoon led by a truly hyperactive hamster who circled us like an angry, furry moon.

"With my life," I said.

She nodded slowly, and I wrapped my tail around her, gently tugging her along.

About a half hour into our walk we found the remnants of what we could only assume was a pack of dogs, perhaps the ones who had attacked Bast's group before Hannah had escaped.

"Torn apart by zombies," Wally said, standing over the tail of a golden retriever. "Poor canines. Never thought I would say that in my lifetime."

Hannah and I had found the ear of a whippet, and she gave it an angry kick. "That's for Tiger!" She snarled at it and stalked off, back on the tracks before I could do more than shiver at her anger. I walked slowly over to Ginger's side; he had avoided investigating what was left of the dogs. I felt a little ill myself. I hoped I never got used to seeing the remnants of a zombie attack.

"So, the zombies will consume an entire dog if they can," I said in a low voice, watching Emmy circle past us before continuing, "but what happens when they bite? Did you ever find out what happened to Vance? Did he turn into a zombie or did he just die?"

Ginger shook his head. "We never saw him again, and Emmy hasn't talked, as you know."

We fell in step behind Hannah, her fur glowing in the sunlight like a beacon, and Ginger poked his whiskers at me. "You landed on your paws, though, didn't you?"

I couldn't help but grin, because he was right, I had. "She's incredible, isn't she?"

"No more so than the cat she hangs out with, but yes," Ginger replied with a wink that was so much his old self I would have laughed aloud but for the obstacle that came into view at that moment. About a mile ahead of us, we could see a large black mouth with boulder-shaped teeth all around it.

"What is it?" I asked in a hushed whisper.

"It's called a tunnel," Trip said, pulling on his whiskers. "Humans burrow through rock and make tunnels. Like moles. So, do we go around it?"

The only moles I knew were the ones Wally's pets cursed for destroying their vegetable garden, but they were burrowing through dirt, not solid rock. The way humans could so dramatically change the world we all shared was astounding. This had been a mountain before the humans had encountered it. And now it was a mountain with a hole that went right through it. What kind of animals could burrow through solid rock?

"Do you see a way around it?" Wally challenged. "There's a mountain on the left and a cliff on the right. And Pickles said the last train went south. This tunnel is directly south."

"Are you sure?" asked Trip, staring at the sky.

Ginger snorted. "Cats always know which direction we're going. From the time we're kittens."

"What do you want to do, Pickles?" Wally asked.

I must have look surprised at the question because he sat back on his haunches and waited for a reply, polishing his bronze star.

"I ... I'm not in charge. I'm sure Ginger could ...," I started to say.

"Oh no," Ginger said, waving a paw in front of me. "This is your mission to find your pet. Like it or not, Pickles, you're leading this expedition."

Wally nodded. "I agree. My pets are adults, and as much as I am worried about them, they are able to take care of themselves. Unlike Connor. So, I ask again, what do you want to do, Pickles?"

I looked at Hannah, who nodded back at me encouragingly.

"I have never been in a tunnel before. What is after the tunnel?" I asked.

"The train tracks should continue through the tunnel and beyond it," Trip said, squinting at the darkness as if he could see the other side. "Like I said, humans use it to get through to somewhere else. They aren't like caves. They don't end. They go through."

"Then I want to keep going. The train took the humans south, and south is through that tunnel," I said, swallowing my doubts.

"All right. Cats aren't afraid of the dark, but hamsters might be," Ginger said, looking at Emmy, who had stopped orbiting us and now sat on her haunches sniffing the air.

"Emmy, you don't have to follow us in there," I said, and then extended that message further. "None of you do. I'm the only one who is committed to finding my pet."

Wally snorted, sliding past me on the tracks to walk straight towards the tunnel, his thick gray tail twitching his opinion loud and clear. Hannah was sticking to me like glue, but Ginger shrugged and followed him, as did Trip, though the raccoon wanted to discuss in detail our options for escape in a tunnel. And who would be in charge of raccoon-saving.

"Emmy?" I repeated. I owed her this much patience. She had helped save us from the zombies at the train car.

She twitched her nose and I tried to decipher her hamster-speech. I was usually very good at foreign languages, but the most I could get from her was that she was still very upset about Vance and Ralph. I had never heard of a hamster attaching itself so strongly to dogs, but perhaps it was the manner of their deaths that had struck her so hard. If nothing, dogs are stupidly loyal. They'll throw themselves in front of their pets, their friends — heck, I once saw a corgi defend a beach towel against a flock of diarrhea-stricken pigeons for three hours. (Again, don't ask.) Ralph's sacrifice would have been honorable to any other dog, but to a hamster, it probably seemed unfathomable.

Finally, she seemed to come to a decision and dropped to all fours, racing ahead of the rest of the troop to lead us into the inky maw ahead.

The tunnel wound its way through the mountain, so by the time we were about a mile in, it was impossible to tell if it was day or night because we could not see any light ahead or behind us. The wind whistled through the tunnel, making sounds that kept my nerves on edge. We were also moving up at a steady rate, climbing the mountain. It was cooler, and despite the fact that we cats could see in here almost as well as we could in sunlight, our group condensed so that I could feel Hannah on my left, Ginger on my right, their whiskers brushing against mine comfortingly. We always knew exactly where Trip was because he kept up a nervous chatter throughout, most of it directed at Wally, who was at the front again now that Emmy had returned to her circling.

Her sight was the weakest, but she kept up her patrol, running into everything from the walls to the tracks to us, and squeaking her protests every time.

"Trip, it's unlikely that you're the last raccoon on Earth," Wally was saying. "Oh, for Saber's sake, Emmy, that was my paw!"

A squeak was her only apology (and truth be told, it sounded more like a swear than an apology to my ears).

Hannah giggled nervously, and the sound echoed through the tunnel. "I know cats aren't supposed to care about the dark, but I hate this."

"Me too," I assured her, glad she'd said it first. It was nice to know that I wasn't the only one. I rubbed my whiskers against her face. "But it has to end sometime."

"Did you get any other information on the pets since I left you?" Ginger asked from my right. "I mean, since that mad opossum?"

"None," I replied, "but I have to hope that we get some clue before the tracks end."

"The other raccoons are probably in hiding," Wally continued to assure Trip. "Weren't you alone when you found Pickles and Ginger?"

"I was," Trip said, "but I know for a fact that I would be bird feed if not for your pretty partner."

I felt Hannah's smile before she purred at me, and felt my heart swell a little more. "One benefit to this forsaken tunnel is that we haven't seen a tail feather of an eagle since entering it."

Ginger nodded, and for a second, I thought he was purring at me too — the whole tunnel seemed to be vibrating suddenly.

That's when Emmy shot by us, knocking Hannah and I apart, screeching at the top of her tiny lungs: "TRAIN! TRAIN! TRAIN!"

I leapt to the left instinctively, calling for my friends to do the same, and felt the whoosh of something very fast fly past me as I hit the wall of the tunnel. The sound was deafening, like a thunderstorm confined to a small space, the echoes threatening to destroy the tiny hairs in my ears. I howled in response, trying to drown out the terror. My claws dug into the wall, and I felt the speed of the train trying to pull me with it. Faintly, I could hear Emmy shrieking, and I wondered what kind of claws hamsters had. Would they be enough? Where was Hannah? The train seemed to go on and on, and just when I felt like I couldn't hold on any longer, it passed and I dropped to the floor of the tunnel, my legs burning with fatigue. The smell of electricity and steel lingered in the air like a cloud created by Thor himself.

"Hannah?" I croaked at the darkness, picking myself up with difficulty, my limbs like jelly. "Wally?"

But it was the hamster of all mammals who crawled out of the darkness, whimpering and lost.

"Emmy," I called to her, and she stopped shuffling long enough for me to put my paws around her and pull her shaking body close. She was moving stiffly, and I licked at her until I found the location of her injury. Her back leg was bleeding, and she hissed when I found the wound.

"Just hold still," I advised, licking the dirt out of the wound. "We'll find something to cover this; you'll be good as new."

I scanned the area around us, hesitant to move forward or back. Surely the rest of our friends were close by? With Emmy hobbling behind me, each step punctuated by a squeak of pain, I made a small circuit, finding a hair elastic and a piece of cloth, once again, a solution provided by the humans who had created them. I could use them to stop the bleeding. I was binding them around the hamster's leg when Wally found us, walking a little dizzily, but in one piece.

"Pickles, thank the Saber-toothed tiger," he said, collapsing at our side. "I thought that opossum said humans took the LAST train."

"Someone didn't get the memo," I replied, "or the mad opossum got his wires crossed along with his brain waves. Who knows? So, that was a train?"

"That was definitely a train. I got knocked into the wall of the tunnel and walked in the wrong direction for who knows how long until I realized I was walking downhill," Wally said. "Basic training saves me again."

"Do you think any of the others are walking back out of the tunnel the wrong way?" I asked, squinting anxious eyes in the direction he had come.

"I don't know," he admitted, taking a look at Emmy's leg, and giving her a comforting lick. "Do you think we should go back or forward?"

I realized they were both looking to me for an answer and I didn't want to admit that I didn't know what we should do. Again. My heart pulled me in two directions — towards Connor at the end of this tunnel and towards Hannah, wherever she was.

"South is that way I believe," Wally said, pointing with his tail.

We waited for as long as I could stomach it, calling out each name again and again, listening to our calls echo back at us. Eventually, with a heavy heart, I got up and restarted our upward exit of the tunnel. Wally and I took turns helping Emmy. We would need to find a better way to transport her, because at this rate, with her hobbling between us, it could take us days to get out of the hellish tunnel.

The silence was stifling, but other than calling out the names of our friends, none of us had the heart to speak. Emmy continued to squeak her distress which I knew would attract our friends if they heard it. I had no sense of how long we walked in that fashion, only that every sound made me turn in hopes of seeing Hannah, Trip, or Ginger, but none appeared.

It was Wally who saw the glow of light at the end of the tunnel, and that sped up our steps, even Emmy found new strength at the prospect of escaping the absolute darkness. We exited the tunnel and immediately got off the tracks, finding a small patch of moss and plunking down in exhaustion.

"Water?" Wally croaked from his prone position, Emmy panting beside him. His fur was matted and messy, which was totally out of character, and his bronze star hidden from view.

"I'll look for some. You keep calling for the others?" I offered, though I was as tired as him.

He nodded, and sat facing the tunnel, repeating the names of our friends.

I pulled myself up and looked at the fir tree above us. I might find something of use up there. I climbed the tree slowly, feeling every inch I gained in my bones. I made it to one of the lower branches, and seeing a squirrel hole, I sniffed at it. No one was home, so I stuck my head in. Mostly nuts, as expected, but also a pile of string and strips of cloth. I pulled both out and tossed them below, hearing Emmy's surprised squeak when they hit the ground. I kept climbing until I ran out of branches, and looked all around.

Ahead I could see the tracks continued, curling their way around the mountainside. The sun was setting soon, we would need to find better shelter than our patch of moss. I could see zombies moving silently in the forests that lined the cliff face, but the angle of the cliff didn't seem to encourage climbing, so we might be safe from that side. I scanned the trees to my left and right and did a double-take, one tree over and about a yard below my vantage point was a suspended platform. It had a roof and a base, and the size made me sure it was human-built rather than squirrel or bird. It looked a little like Connor's tree house in our backyard, only with fewer walls and no toys. Humans again, changing the environment to suit their needs. Amazing.

I carefully climbed from my tree to the floor of this platform, which was only ten feet off the ground. The dimensions were right for a human, and there was wiring stuck through the wood. I pulled on it steadily, hoping it was not electrified, and getting enough of it out to drop it to the forest floor below.

With Wally's help, I tied the wires around Emmy,

and hoisted her up into the roofed platform. She squeaked in protest, but settled in nicely once she was up. Water had pooled in a small mug on the corner of the platform, so we sated our thirst and then Wally and I curled around Emmy. Soon, their breathing slowed into a steady rhythm of sleep. I couldn't close my eyes, they were locked on the tunnel we had escaped, looking for any sign of the rest of our friends.

DAY TWENTY-SEVEN

"Are you sure?" Wally asked again.

"I have to try," I answered, flicking water off my whiskers. We had woken to a drizzle of rain that had quickly turned to a deluge. Our treehouse didn't have walls, but the roof was doing a decent job of keeping us dry. Damp, if you wanted to be accurate. Have I mentioned where water sits on a cat's list of worst enemies?

"Be careful," Wally advised, pushing the mug under a dripping leak to collect more water, "and stay off the tracks themselves. We'll wait for you here. If you're not back by sundown, I'm coming in after you. Standard protocol."

I had brought up some more sticks and the string

and cloth I had dropped from the squirrel's nest. In my absence, Wally was going to try and construct something he called a travois — a military invention used for transporting wounded soldiers — to haul our wounded hamster.

I leapt down onto the muddy forest floor and scampered back into the tunnel. I immediately started calling for Hannah, Trip, and Ginger. I made my way down the first curve, losing the cloudy daylight behind me. I would be the first to admit that I have abandonment issues, but I think you would agree, I was dealing with them well. Or as well as could be expected under the circumstances of losing everyone I ever cared about. Connor seemed so far away right now that I couldn't let myself think of him.

My steps were near silent as I walked close to the tunnel wall, taking my time, scanning every dark corner for a glimpse of my friends. My worst nightmare would be to find their broken bodies, but I wouldn't turn away: I had to know their fates. Not knowing was so much worse.

The second worst nightmare was the sound I heard coming my way: the sound of groaning and dragging that I associated with zombies. Nowhere to hide, I froze in place, wondering if zombies could see in the dark. Wondering if they could see at all out of those dead eyeballs. I was ready to turn tail and race out the way

I had come when I realized I recognized those grunts.

"Trip!" I whispered, as the raccoon came into sight around a bend in the tunnel. My joy was tempered with the realization of what, or who, he was dragging.

I sprinted to his side, but he barely noticed, and I could see why: he had a deep cut in his forehead and was weaving about like an over-nipped old tabby. In each paw was a cat leg I recognized — one for Hannah and one for Ginger — thankfully still attached to their bodies.

"Trip," I said softly, trying to stop his forward motion, "let me help you."

He turned confused eyes my way and I realized he was operating on pure instinct, dragging his friends to safety with no other plan than to get them out of this tunnel.

I stopped him and examined the two cats. They were both breathing, bruised, and had cuts all over their bodies. Trip slowed down, but wouldn't stop so I poked him in the belly. For the first time since we'd met, he growled at me, his ears flattening against his head. I jumped back in shock.

"Trip, it's me, Pickles," I said in the softest voice I could. "I need your help, my friend. Can you carry Ginger? I will carry Hannah. We need to get out of this tunnel."

He didn't seem to understand, just pushed me out of the way — teeth bared — and picked up our friends by their feet and continued to drag them. Deciding to help him rather than fight, I did my best to lift their heads out of the way of rocks and garbage and we painstakingly made our way out of the tunnel. At the exit, Trip dropped their feet and promptly fell flat on his face, unconscious. He had spent the last of his strength and I would never be able him to repay him for it.

"Wally," I yelled, patting Hannah's face, trying to revive her.

But instead of Wally's face, twenty-five chipmunks looked down at us from the platform above.

"Who's Wally?" asked one of them.

"I ... well, that is ...," I answered, my brain trying to work in the driving rain with my friends scattered at my feet.

"Is he the fat one or the squeaky one?" the chipmunk asked, prompting some muffled squeaks from somewhere behind him. They sounded like they were coming from an agitated hamster, and I just happened to be missing one of those.

"Listen, do you think we could talk somewhere out of the rain?" I yelled up to him, wiping water out of my eyes.

"We're all full at the inn," the chipmunk said, "but if you go back in that tunnel, we will come down and palaver."

It sounded like this chipmunk read the same books

I did, and what choice did I really have? Leap up the tree and take on dozens of chipmunks on my own?

I nodded and started dragging Hannah back into the shelter of the tunnel. When I had her tucked into the edge, I turned back for Ginger, but he had struggled to his feet.

"I think I got hit by a train," said Ginger, slurring slightly. "What did I miss?"

"Pack of chipmunks took our treehouse," I whispered, grabbing one of Trip's feet and dragging him towards Hannah, "and I think they've got Wally and Emmy up there."

"We have a treehouse?" Ginger asked, taking Trip's other leg and helping me.

"Had," I underlined grimly, keeping one eye on the dozens of eyes watching us from above.

Ginger started licking Trip. "I woke up at some point," he said, shaking his head and then wincing at the pain that brought on. "I thought I saw Trip wandering around, bumping into walls."

I nodded miserably, licking Hannah's ear, still looking for a wound that would explain her continued unconsciousness. She had a big lump over her right eye that worried me, and I had no idea how to treat it.

"Look out!" exclaimed Trip, scaring us both as he sat up suddenly. Then he grabbed at his head. "Whoa, I feel like I got hit by a train."

"He's back," Ginger said, turning to examine Hannah next. "One more to go."

"Plus the ones up there," I said, nervously looking up at the platform where the little chipmunk heads had disappeared from sight.

"So, what's our plan with the chipmunks?" Ginger asked, licking at Hannah, his worry coming off his whiskers in vibrations.

I couldn't let my own fears for Hannah override the near and present danger Wally and Emmy might be in.

"I'd prefer not to fight, but if it comes to it …," I said watching three chipmunks descend from the treehouse, "then we fight."

"Fight? Okay," Trip repeated, raising his paws like he was Muhammad Ali, a human boxer Wally's pet seemed to worship. "Who are we fighting?"

"Maybe you should watch Hannah, Trip," Ginger suggested, stepping to my side as the chipmunks scampered into the mouth of the tunnel.

"Now, you were asking after a Wally," the head chipmunk said, nodding at the chipmunk to his left, who pulled out a tiny notebook and an even tinier pencil. The head chipmunk had a magnificent white moustache that curled perfectly at the ends. It shouldn't surprise you that he couldn't seem to stop twirling the thing. The secretary chipmunk was small and wiry with black spots all over his body, and the third chipmunk was the size of Emmy, and had his arms crossed over his large chest, so I guessed he was the "muscle," such as he was.

"We're not looking for 'a Wally,' we're looking for our friend whose name is Wally," I corrected, trying not to be distracted by the chipmunk scribbling in front of me. "He's a gray cat and he was up on that platform caring for our other friend, a hamster named Emmy."

"Ah, so now you are looking to get an Emmy and a Wally. Make sure you get that down Carl," said the head chipmunk imperiously.

"Carl, could you also maybe tell us if you have a Wally and an Emmy who fit the descriptions of our friends?" asked Ginger in a saccharine voice.

I suggested he knock off the sarcasm with my whiskers, but the chipmunks seemed to take his question seriously.

"Oh, as soon as we know what you have to trade with, my fine feline, we will enumerate our goods for trade. Now, I count three normal-sized felines and one extra-large feline wearing a mask. Carl, make a note," the head chipmunk said.

"Trade?" I repeated, confused. "You want us to trade for our friends like property?"

The chipmunks looked at each other like it was obvious. "Well, of course," Carl answered, earning a glare from his leader. "That is the purpose of a palaver."

The leader cleared his throat, bringing our attention back to him. "If this is not a trade, then we will return to our nest, we have many other animals to do business with."

They started to turn away and I could feel Ginger getting ready to pounce and end negotiations with blood, when Trip called out, "We want to trade, oh wise sir. Let us gather our goods and make an offer."

My mouth dropped open at his suggestion, but the chipmunks simply nodded graciously and bounded back up the tree to the platform.

HANNAH WOKE UP as I was spooning water into her mouth with my paw. The rain had finally receded, which made sense, because Hannah was awake and she required the sun to glow.

I was so relieved I started to cry, and she licked my cheeks as I explained our situation.

She was dizzy and had a migraine of a headache, but she stood up and walked around, testing her limbs with success. Her fur on the top of her head and back had been rubbed almost down to the skin from Trip's dragging rescue, but otherwise, she was remarkably all right.

"So, where are Trip and Ginger?" she asked after lapping water from the discarded bottle cap I had filled in the rain last night.

"According to Trip, trade negotiation with chipmunks

is all about the drama and spectacle and less about the actual items themselves."

"So, his plan is to make a big deal about garbage he finds in this tunnel and trade that for Wally and Emmy's lives?" she asked doubtfully.

"I know, it's nuts," I said, shaking my head, "but it's the only plan we've got."

"Maybe not the only plan," she said, her whiskers resonating with an idea. "You said they called Trip an extra-large feline?"

Trip and Ginger returned about a half hour later to find us curled up in a contented ball of purring and planning.

"Ahem," said Ginger as they approached, his eyes able to see in the dark better than Trip's.

I stood up. "Tell me you found something."

Ginger was already shaking his head, but Trip was excited, bouncing on the tips of his feet. "Did we ever!" He shook a plastic bag of things our way. "Let's get this palaver going!"

He walked straight out into the sunlight and called up to Carl, announcing that we were ready. I looked over my shoulder at Hannah, who nodded and walked farther into the tunnel to curl up in a ball.

"She's awake," Ginger said, glancing back at her. "Is she all right?"

"She's better than all right," I said with a nervous shake of my tail. "Follow our lead."

Five chipmunks came down out of the tree this time, including the leader we had met before, the secretary Carl, and three more of the bulky bodyguard chipmunks.

The leader's eyes lit up seeing the bag of goodies in Trip's paw and he stopped in front of him, signaling to Carl to bring out his notes.

"Good day, felines. Shall we go over the minutes from our last meeting?" he asked, pressing his paws together.

"Yes, please," said Trip politely, mimicking the leader's stance.

"A trade for one Wally and one Emmy was proposed by the right honorable Kimchi the second," Carl read from his notes, nodding at the leader. The rest of the chipmunks in the treehouse were hanging on every word, their chubby faces pointed down at us, their eyes locked on Trip's bag.

"We would like to add to that offer," Kimchi said, twirling his 'stache towards Hannah and eliciting a unified gasp from his audience of chipmunks. "We have three healers in our community who would be happy to take a look at your damaged feline over there."

Hannah picked up her head, giving a small meow of pain.

"We would welcome the help," I said, nodding at Carl to add it to his list.

Kimchi beamed and rubbed his little paws together.

This mammal was a tiny caricature of Disney villains. "Now, what do you offer in trade?"

Trip waved his paws over the plastic bag dramatically. "Prepare to be astounded, chipmunks, as I present the spoon of Abalone!"

He carefully removed a plastic spoon from the bag, using only two fingers to handle it. "Used by only the most refined of mammals to carry items long distances, this spoon of Abalone was passed through generations to get to you."

Kimchi's eyes were the size of saucers as he reached for the plastic spoon and Trip reminded him twice to be careful with it before gently passing it on to him. The rest of the chipmunks gathered round the spoon, ooohing and aaahing, and Carl held his pencil poised over his tiny notebook, waiting for judgment.

Kimchi finally nodded imperiously at Carl, who quickly scratched something onto his pad. Ginger threw an incredulous look my way, but I flicked my tail at Trip. This show was far from over.

"I wonder if I should …," Trip said, looking into his bag of goodies. "No, I shouldn't. But this!"

He pulled out a marble the size of his hand. "This orb of destiny is rare and worthy of trade."

He placed it on the ground between his feet and those of the chipmunks. "It foretold our destiny of meeting you here, and I know of fewer than five in existence!"

The chipmunks stared down at the marble in wonder. "How does it work?" one of them asked in a hushed tone.

Trip looked to Kimchi with a secretive smile. "This is a very powerful orb, oh great Kimchi. Perhaps its powers are not for all members of your group."

That started a squabble, the chipmunks descending into squeaks and arguments, Carl frantically trying to keep up with his notes. Two chipmunks on the platform above started fighting and fell off the platform into our midst, much to the chagrin of Kimchi.

"Please!" he chirped at his brethren. "Calm yourselves! We will add an addendum to this transaction for a sub-negotiation on the use of the ...." He looked to Trip for help.

"Orb of destiny," Trip supplied with a low bow.

"Yes, Carl, please add that to the minutes," Kimchi said, his paws making grabby motions towards the marble.

Carl scratched the appropriate notes with no less than five chipmunks reading over his shoulder to make sure the minutes reflected their lobbying.

"Finally, my fair and reasonable chipmunks, I offer this invaluable weapon for your defense," Trip announced in a booming voice, all eyes turning back to him. "This is the sword of ... Shakira!"

He pulled out a small plastic sword, the kind humans used at parties to spear, well, pickles and other small food items. This one was blue and glinted in the sunlight as Trip held it aloft.

Another appreciative gasp went up from the group of chipmunks and I heard a squeak from the platform. I coughed to cover the sound, and Ginger looked at me curiously, but none of the other chipmunks seemed to notice; the sword had their full attention.

With a final flourish, Trip stabbed the sword into the soft ground at his feet.

Kimchi looked from Carl to the items in front of Trip with naked greed in his eyes.

"You honor us with this trade, felines," he said finally, signaling to his brethren to silence, "and for these items, we are willing to offer you one Wally and the service of one healer for your damaged cat."

He again pointed towards the ball of gold curled inside the tunnel.

"And what about Emmy?" growled Ginger through his teeth.

Kimchi turned to confer with his band, and Ginger's tail began to snap against me. He wanted to attack so badly his twitching tail was sending off sparks of static every time it touched me.

I knew Kimchi was going to deny us before he turned around, in fact, I'd assumed it from the moment he'd proposed the trade.

"I'm sorry my feline friends," he said finally, looking

anything but sorry, "but unless you have more items to trade …."

Trip threw a desperate look my way, so I stepped forward. "We do, honorable Kimchi."

Kimchi's surprise was immediately replaced by that familiar look of greed I had come to expect from him.

"Oh?" he asked, waving impatiently at Carl to pick up his pencil again, twirling his moustache anew.

"Yes, we have fourteen …," I glanced up at the platform, "sorry, fifteen chipmunks to trade as well."

Kimchi looked confused. His beady eyes flicked from me to the empty plastic bag in Trip's paws and then back to me.

Ginger grinned for the first time since being hit by the train, his eyes locked on the platform above. The chipmunks finally followed his gaze to see a glorious Abyssinian standing over a bundle of trussed-up chipmunks. Wally was standing at attention, his bronze medal gleaming around his neck as he glared down at them, and Emmy traced limping circles from the roof.

DAY TWENTY-EIGHT

"I would have loved to see a transcript of those minutes," I said as soon as we were out of earshot of the chipmunks. We left them in the midst of loudly electing a new leader. Kimchi was in tears and taking the brunt of their failure to negotiate a winning hand. Carl was alternating between consoling him and smacking him with his tiny notebook.

"It was a pile of leaves?" Trip kept repeating at Hannah, walking beside her. "You hid behind a pile of leaves and then snuck out, and they didn't even notice?"

"You didn't notice," Wally pointed out, taking his turn pulling Emmy's tiny travois, "and their eyesight is much weaker than yours."

"Hey, Trip was busy giving the performance of a lifetime," Hannah said, patting the raccoon on the back. "I've never heard anything like it."

Trip pulled at his whiskers. "I don't think I've ever been more surprised than when I looked up to see what you had done to those chipmunks."

"We!" squeaked Emmy from her travois.

Emmy's voice had returned for good and it was laced with well-earned pride. Hannah had climbed up the back of the tree and cut Emmy's bonds first. It was she who had cowed the chipmunks into shocked silence as Hannah released Wally. Then the three of them trussed up the mammals in a bundle of fur and shocked faces and waited to see the results of our negotiations below.

"This is going to make for the best story," Ginger said, his grin wide. "No one is going to believe me."

"We will," said Emmy.

We rounded a bend in the tracks and I stopped suddenly. "Do you see that?"

Hannah squinted where I was pointing, and then her eyes flew wide. "Is that …?"

"It's a zombie tied to a tree!" said Trip, pulling at his whiskers so hard one came free in his paw. He looked down at it distractedly, and then placed it in the plastic bag he was still dragging around. Waste not, want not.

We gave the undead human a large berth, walking on the other side of the tracks and keeping it in full view.

It caught sight or scent or whatever it used to track the living when we were about ten yards from it, turning its gnashing face in our direction and redoubling its efforts to get loose.

"Someone cut off its arms and legs," Ginger said, revulsion obvious in his tail. "Why didn't they kill it rather than tie it up like this?"

"He's a message!" I said, excited. "Look!"

An arrow was painted on the zombie's wasted chest. We followed the arrow away from the frustrated dead human to a Tupperware box half buried in the ground. Trip wrestled the lid open to find a hand-written note that I carefully unfolded.

"What does it say?" Wally asked.

"It's a list of names," I answered, my heart beating fast as I scanned it. "Connor's name is on it!"

"What about my pets?" demanded Wally.

"Yes! They are both on here as well!" I said, smiling at Wally, who released the breath he had been holding.

"It says this group of humans passed the night here and are moving up the mountain to something called a safe house. They write that it is isolated and hard to access and therefore the zombies will have trouble getting to it."

"Well, that's good, isn't it Pickles?" Hannah said. "Why aren't you smiling?"

I had reached the end of the note by now and gave

it back to Trip to replace in the Tupperware before answering. "They warn that they will be leaving traps along the way so as to stop any zombies who might follow."

"Traps?" Ginger said, backing up from the Tupperware and scanning the distance.

"I see another zombie," Wally said, pulling our attention to a dirt road leading away from the train tracks.

Sure enough, tied to another tree was a second armless, legless zombie.

"No message?" Hannah said, circling the zombie, who strained against the chains wrapped around her.

"I think the message in this case is 'follow us up this path if your brains still work,'" Wally said.

"Why are they using zombies as messages?" Ginger asked, still looking a little green from all the missing limbs.

"Maybe it throws the zombies off their trail?" Hannah suggested. "We still don't know what senses they use to track the living, but if it's smell, the smell of these dead things might cover the smell of live humans."

"We'd need a dog to test that theory, but it's a good one," Wally agreed, looking up the road to see the arms and legs of these two unfortunate creatures scattered in our path.

"Traps?" Emmy reminded us helpfully from her travois.

"Traps," I repeated, Wally taking the lead position and walking up the road away from the zombies.

We walked for an hour in the glorious sunlight before we ran across the first trap. The humans had cut down and sharpened about thirty tree branches and jammed them into the earth, angled towards us like spears. We were looking up at it, discussing whether it would actually work when a teenage zombie offered an effective demonstration, coming out of the trees and scaring us with his silent attack. Trip screeched like an eagle and slid between the spear-like branches before we could do more than leap away, and the teenager followed him, impaling himself on two of the sharpened ends and reaching out with his arms towards the raccoon.

"Trip!" I yelled. "Stop!" The raccoon was running pell-mell down the road and out of our sight.

"I'll get him," Ginger called as he took off after Trip. I looked up at the teenaged zombie, who was now reaching for me, but unable to disengage from the thick branches in his torso. Hannah slid through the branches as far away from the zombie as she could, pulling Emmy behind her in the travois. "It stopped him, but do you think he will work his way off?"

Wally and I followed her through and walked another six feet before looking back at the situation. If anything, the zombie was pushing himself further onto the branches as he reached for us, moaning and snapping his jaws.

"As a physical deterrent, it's effective for one or two of those things," Wally said finally, "but a herd of them would push the first soldier onto the branches and then push through them with their added weight."

A few ravens dipped out of the sky, circling our position, so we turned away from the groaning dead human and continued on our way. This part of the outside world was very different from the city. It seemed to have less human-ness to it. The trees lined the path, the dirt had not been covered up by pavement and the air just sniffed cleaner. Interesting. Maybe I was beginning to like the world outside the human-made boxes just a little bit.

"Traps." Emmy reminded us again solemnly, and we all nodded, between the silent attack and the first trap, we needed to stay on high alert.

We saw Ginger and Trip sitting on the side of the road and overheard a bit of their conversation as we rejoined them. Trip seemed quite embarrassed about how fast and far he had run from the skewered zombie, and Ginger, in very un-Ginger-like fashion, was doing his best to reassure the raccoon that no one was judging him.

Instead of joining the conversation at all, I offered to take over pulling Emmy. "Trip, can you detach Emmy from Hannah? I can take her for a little while."

Trip quietly did as I asked and then walked beside me as I brought up the rear of our small fellowship.

"I think I have to find a way to fight zombies on my own," he said finally, "like you cats do. You never seem scared."

"Well, then we're doing a great job of hiding it," I said.

He looked surprised and I said, "I'm terrified. All the time. Of losing Connor's trail. Of losing one of you. Of losing all of you and being alone. This is my first time outside of a house in my whole life, and you have to admit, it's not exactly ideal."

Trip's eyebrows came together, which on the face of a raccoon with a mask looks quite sinister. "How do I stop the fear from taking over?"

"I don't know, I'm just learning on the fly," I said, laughing at the idea that I could give advice on how to be brave, "and you've been doing incredibly well. That whole deal with the chipmunks? We could never have done that without you."

"I was ready to shred those little rats," Ginger growled from a few steps ahead of us. "I still might if I see that Kimchi character again."

"We had a family of chipmunks living in our tree," explained Trip, "and every Friday was the neighborhood trade night. They'd host it at different trees, and when it was held in our tree, you could hear the negotiations late into the night. Always sounded more like something on a stage than an auction."

"Ridiculous creatures," grumbled Wally, who was leading the group, casting his eyes left and right for traps. Always count on Wally to take his responsibilities seriously.

"You understand this human-made world more than any cat I've met," said Hannah, "and we're the ones assigned to protect them."

Trip shrugged before speaking. "They're a crazy species. They waste almost as much as they create. I don't understand them, never have. But you don't have to understand a mammal to learn from them, and I learned a lot from humans ... and chipmunks, come to think of it.

"My family hated those neighborhood trading nights," Trip continued. "They'd head out on garbage patrol when the trade was in our tree, but I would stay behind and listen. Never thought I'd get the chance to participate."

The mention of Trip's family quieted us all down as we thought of those we'd never see again, and those we were fighting so hard to find. I had just opened my mouth to ask Emmy about Vance's last days when Trip suddenly started sniffing the air.

"What? More zombies?" Wally said, stopping and signaling everyone else to do the same.

Now all our noses were in the air, but I was catching nothing.

"No," Trip whispered, turning this way and that. "Food!"

Ginger grabbed Trip's tail in both his paws. "Okay, but let's go slowly. Remember. Traps."

"Why would humans leave food as traps?" Hannah whispered. "Do zombies eat food?"

I shook my head. "I don't think so, and if it was actual food, wouldn't we smell it too? Trip, are you smelling food or garbage?"

He looked at me confused and I realized, he really didn't know the difference. All garbage was food, and all food was ... well, food.

"I don't like it," Wally said, watching Trip zone in on the location of the food/garbage.

"It's this way!" Trip whispered, dragging Ginger off the road, his tail still firmly in his grip.

We followed, cautiously, still sniffing the air for whatever Trip was following.

"Up there!" he said, finally, pointing at a plastic bag hanging from a tree.

"I'm liking this less and less," Wally said, looking up at the bag.

I agreed, and walked a few steps forward to where Trip was straining against Ginger's hold. "Trip, we'll find food, but let's find it ourselves rather than ... like this. It's too convenient."

"Convenient?" Trip repeated, looking down at me

like I was speaking Latin. "It's human food hauled up into a tree so that scavengers can't get ahold of it. Haven't you ever been camping?"

I snorted at the insult. Cats do not camp.

"I sniff rabbit scat nearby," Hannah said helpfully. "I'm sure between the five of us ...."

"Six!" Emmy announced.

"Between the six of us, we can capture a few for dinner," she finished.

I didn't correct her, but there was no way I would be any help in capturing dinner.

"But ... just a little?" Trip begged, his eyes dilated as he looked up at the bag like it was sent by angels and unicorns rather than discarded by desperate humans.

"No," said Wally with finality, stalking around the edge of the small clearing, "I have assessed the situation and I will not risk ...."

He never finished his sentence, because in the next second our world became reduced to a tight bag of leaves, sticks, hissing cats, a drooling raccoon, and a very angry hamster.

DAY TWENTY-NINE

"This is just like that movie!"

"Shut up, Trip."

"The one with the small bears with spears who wore hoods and ...."

"We KNOW, Trip."

I had a mouthful of net, trying to bite through the fabric, or I would have answered the raccoon, and probably not with a polite word. I was upside down with my legs sticking straight up, one leg all the way through the netting as I chewed as hard as I could.

"Pickles," Hannah's voice said from somewhere above me.

I pushed the net out of my mouth for a second. "What?"

"Grab Emmy."

I tried to turn my face, but all the mammals on top of me made it impossible. "I can't see her."

"Trip, roll my way," I heard Ginger's voice say, and I felt a slight easing of the weight, enough so that I could turn my head a little bit. That's when I saw what Hannah was concerned about: Emmy's wiggling butt was hanging out of the netting. In fact, from this angle, I couldn't see what was keeping the hamster in this net with the rest of us.

"Are you holding on to Emmy, Hannah?" I called, reaching my one free leg towards the mammal, and not even coming close.

"Yes, but she's slipping!"

I looked down, judged the distance, and said, "Let her go. At least one of us will be free of this net. It's not too far for her to drop."

"Let go," repeated Emmy plaintively.

"Are you sure?" Hannah asked.

I heard stirring in the bushes and said, "Let her go. Now!"

Emmy dropped to the ground below me, landing on her side (no cat DNA in that animal), and scampered to a hole at the base of a tree just as three humans entered the glade.

"What did we get, Hussein?" said one to the other, looking up at us in the net.

The one named Hussein walked up so he was directly under me, and I fought the urge to hiss, pulling my leg back into the netting.

He grabbed the net bag and twisted it this way and that. "A bunch of cats and ... a raccoon, I think! Weird!"

The other two humans came up to stand under the net beside him, all three now looking up at us.

"They don't look bitten," I said.

"Let's take them back to camp," Hussein said, walking over to the tree to untie the other end of the rope. "Who's got the bag?"

"Bag?" Hannah whispered. "I'm not going in a bag."

"Me neither," Trip swore.

"What if Connor is with these humans?" I said, desperate but scared.

"Then we follow them back to their camp on our own paws," Wally said.

I couldn't disagree with that logic. "Okay, what's the plan?"

"We bite, claw, get free," Ginger said through gritted teeth.

"Climb a tree, as high as you can, and stay within sight of this glade," Wally said as a hand reached into the net and all hell broke loose.

We clawed, hissed, fought, bit, and generally caused

as much mayhem as five mammals with a combined weight of less than ninety pounds could in the small space. I heard the squeals of my friends and bit harder and hissed louder.

"What the hell?"

"Are they rabid!?"

"Ouch! Can raccoons be zombies?!"

"Help me!"

I was free first, and I sprinted away from the humans, leaping up the tree in front of me, climbing and climbing until I was at least ten feet off the ground before I looked back down.

The humans were still cursing, but each was holding a sack of squirming mammals.

"No," I whispered, looking around at the tree branches in the grove with horror. I couldn't have been the only one to escape.

"Leave it," Hussein said, looking up at me and then down at his scratched arm with disgust. "More trouble than it's worth. Damn cat!"

I hissed from my tree branch. "Let them go, you monsters!"

"Pickles!" Hannah called from one of the sacks, breaking my heart. "Help!"

"No," called Wally from a different sack as the humans started to walk away. "Stick to the plan! Pickles, get Emmy and follow us."

"Pickles, don't leave us," Trip caterwauled as he was carried away.

I climbed down from the tree, so scared and angry my claws refused to recede into my paws. "Emmy," I hissed. "Emmy."

"Here," she called from the tree root, only emerging so far that I could see her snout wiggling in the darkness.

"Come on," I said, turning to follow the humans. I would have preferred to follow them through the tree branches, but I knew that wasn't an option with a hamster. Their climbing skills were minimal and Emmy was still injured anyway.

Instead we slunk from tree trunk to tree trunk, moving only fast enough to keep the humans in sight.

"Plan?" Emmy whispered, when we had been following in this manner for about ten minutes.

"Why do I always have to come up with the plan?" I answered grumpily, scampering to the next tree.

We made three more quick darts before Emmy answered: "Connor."

I swallowed past my guilt with effort. It was my fault, my quest, that had gotten us into this much trouble. She was right.

"Fine, sorry," I said finally, grumpier than I meant to sound. "We get to the human camp, rescue our friends, and find Connor."

That's when the herd of zombies attacked. I saw

them first this time, and grabbed Emmy by the nape of her neck, ignoring her squeak of protest, throwing her towards a gap in the roots of the tree in front of us and diving in after her. A zombie grabbed me by the tail and I hissed, digging my claws into the wood of the tree. Emmy streaked past me with a warrior's scream.

"Don't bite it!" I yelled, but I needn't have worried. Emmy's strategy of dodging and dashing through the legs of zombies was incredibly effective. He let my tail go to try and grab at her and she sprinted back into the hole under the roots of the tree. I seized her, scooted as far back as I could, and held her close. No matter how far he reached into the roots under the tree, he couldn't reach us. I closed my eyes against the terror, glad I had Emmy in my paws. The zombie seemed to come to the same conclusion a few terrifying minutes later. He pulled back and rejoined his groaning party chasing the humans. I whispered at Emmy through chattering teeth, "Stay here."

I climbed back out of the gap and up the tree trunk as fast as I could, leaping from branch to branch, above the heads of the herd of moaning zombies. I could see the humans were running as well, the sacks slung over their shoulders as they evaded their dead peers.

I couldn't lose them! I jumped from tree branch to tree branch, moving so fast I barely saw my next landing spot. Mid-air, the world slowed as I saw one of the humans swing at a zombie with a long sword, decapitating it, and that's when the thin branch I landed on cracked underneath me. I fell to the ground and knew no more.

I'M NOT SURE what pulled me from my unconscious state first, Emmy prodding at my tail, or the faint hooting near my ear.

"Emmy, stop. Please," I mumbled, rubbing at my head. I was pretty sure I had landed on it despite making fun of Emmy's earlier landing. In my defense, I was chasing zombies who were chasing humans who had my friends in sacks.

I tried to stand up and fell back on my side, causing a new flurry of hoots.

"What in the Saber?" I said, poking a weirdly shaped pile of leaves underneath me. Only it wasn't leaves. It was an upside-down nest.

I flipped over the nest to find a small brown owl, a chick really, about the size of Emmy, hooting up at me.

"You've got to be kidding," I said to the chick as two large tears rolled out of its big round eyes.

"Kidding," repeated Emmy, shaking her head at the bird.

"Not kidding," said the chick in a deep voice.

I jumped back in surprise. This owl was older than he looked and could speak a common language.

"I don't have time for this," I said to Emmy. "I don't know if this bird is dangerous to hamsters. Emmy, do you need me to kill it?"

The owl looked offended, which made sense of course, and more tears started leaking out of his eyes, but Emmy shook her head immediately. Good, because I wasn't sure how to kill it.

I needed to find which way the humans went, so I climbed the tree nearest to me. Nothing, in any direction. I called out for Hannah. For Wally. For Ginger and for Trip. My meows died in the air. I was no tracker. How was I going to find them, or Connor?

"What are you looking for?" said a deep voice behind me, and I whipped around, claws ready. It was the owl.

"How? What?" I said, looking stupidly at the bird, and then back down at Emmy, so far below us.

"Emmy says you are looking for something," the owl said, taking two tries to settle on my branch with me. It was weird hearing such a deep voice coming from so small an animal, very weird.

"My friends. They were thrown into bags by three humans," I said desperately, scanning the horizon of tree tops. "There were zombies, a whole herd. I can't even see them ...."

Instead of answering, the owl took off into the sky, flying out of my sight quickly.

I climbed back down, my eyes on the sky.

Emmy was waiting for me, pacing in her usual circles. "He's Runt. He's alone too," she said, speaking the most words in a row I'd ever heard her say.

"Can we believe him?" I asked, my neck starting to feel sore from staring up at the sky. "Because an adult owl, say his angry mama, would be a tough fight for just the two of us."

"She abandoned me," the owl said as he descended, sliding to a stop that included a half-roll. "A month ago. She and my brothers and sisters left me for sunnier skies."

Before I could do more than glance at Emmy quizzically, the owl continued. "I see the dead ones in a pile close by."

"Lead us there," I said.

The owl took off, flying a few yards off the ground, close enough for us to follow. Emmy and I took off after him, and just as he said, less than a mile away was a pile of zombies. The owl lifted into the sky as Emmy and I approached the pile cautiously on the ground.

"These humans are skilled at killing zombies," I said, looking carefully at the carcasses as we circled the pile, trying to ignore the smell and the oozing. "I count twelve zombies, killed by three humans."

Emmy had circled the pile three times in the time it took me to do one circuit. "All dead. Not regular dead. Totally dead."

"And no sacks at all," I said, looking up at the sky.

"RUNT!" I yelled.

"Don't think he likes that name," Emmy said, following me into another glade where we could once again see sky between the trees.

"OWL!" I yelled again.

He circled our glade and came in for a stumbling landing.

I sensed that his weird landings were a sore spot for him, so instead I said, "We need your help, friend."

"Friend?" he repeated, cocking his head in that weird way owls do, all big eyes and non-existent necks.

"Friend," I said, pointing at Emmy and myself. "We would be your friends."

"Don't know what this word 'friend' is," the owl said. "Is it like family? Does that mean you're leaving?"

Emmy shook her head at him. "It means we never, ever leave you."

At first, I thought he still didn't understand, and then his eyes filled again and he started sobbing anew, hiding his face under his wing. It took us a full ten minutes to calm the creature down, and another five to explain the whole friendship idea again. Finally, he sat back so that his weird, spindly legs disappeared beneath his voluminous feathers, his tears spent.

"Listen, now that we're friends, I need your help with something," I said, doing everything I could not to restart the waterworks. "Our friends. The ones in the sacks. We think the humans were taking them to a camp nearby."

Runt shook his head again, and I sighed. This owl had never ventured from his nest.

Emmy announced she was going to scrounge for food, so I carefully explained the difference between a human and a zombie, what a camp looked like, and what the heck a sack was. This was a weird position to be in because usually other mammals were explaining the outside world to me.

By the time she got back to us, the sun had set. Emmy had eaten her fill of small insects, but carried a few handfuls back for the owl, who set to eating them immediately. Despite my desperation to get back on the trail of the humans, I took a moment to hunt a bit myself, catching two small mice arguing over a nut, and considered eating them. Thankfully they noticed me and took off, so I settled for a couple mouthfuls of ants, though I really didn't like the way they wiggled on my tongue. The mice would have been worse. I missed food you didn't have to kill. Oh, for the convenience of the convenience store filled with food that humans nicely packaged into bags labeled with an adorable kitten face.

I found Emmy snoring in a hollow at the foot of a tree, a small nest of grass and leaves beneath her.

"Thank you," I said to the owl, sure this was his handiwork.

"I will go and find the camp now, friend Pickles," he

said, spreading his wings. "You rest here with Emmy."

"Wait, before you go," I said, "what shall I call you?"

He seemed to hesitate, so I clarified. "Emmy didn't think the name you gave her was one you liked. Since the only animals who called you by that name are gone, I thought this might be a chance to start over. With a new name."

I'd never spoken to an owl before, so I couldn't be sure what was happening with his beak, but two little dimples appeared in the feathers on either side of his mouth, which could have been his version of a smile. Truthfully, I was just glad he wasn't in tears again.

"How about Pallas?" I suggested. "After Athena, who valued wise owls above all other animals. We could call you Pal for short."

Emmy snorted in her sleep and murmured "Pal."

"Pal," he repeated, testing the word. And then he nodded and took off on his mission.

I paced around Emmy for the first two hours, unwilling to close my eyes in this forest. I kept looking up at the star-filled sky, hoping against hope to see our new friend coming back towards us. I was filled with guilt, and scared that I would lose the trail of my friends and of Connor, but at least I wasn't entirely alone.

I dragged a few loose branches over the hole she slept in and climbed up to the lowest branches of the tree where I could see zombies coming, should they wander into this grove.

DAY THIRTY

A gunshot woke me, and I sprang up in alarm, hearing Emmy do the same below me. I only knew it was a gunshot because of all the cop shows Connor's parents watched, and in real life it is so much louder.

"Pickles?" she cried out, and I leapt down to her side.

"I'm here," I said, staring up at the sky. Were the humans being attacked by zombies?

Gunshots were something I could follow, though. "Come on, Emmy," I said. "Grab my tail. I can lead you in the dark."

We took off between the trees, Emmy holding lightly to the tip of my tail with her teeth, heading towards the receding echo of the sound. I sniffed at the air and found the acrid smell of ammonia and sourness. Is that what a gunshot smells like?

"Traps," Emmy said from behind me, dropping my tail for a second to remind me of the danger.

I nodded, doing my best to continue my tracking while looking for disturbances in the grass that might indicate another net ready to grab us or something worse. Fifteen minutes passed and though the sound was gone, the ammonia smell was still there, and I could hear the voices of humans, so I knew we were getting close to the camp.

I slowed down, dropping my shoulders so I could sneak to the edge of the camp.

All around the humans had stacked sharpened logs in the same manner as the one we had run into earlier, and a few zombies lurched and fought against the wood that skewered their bodies. We picked a spot that didn't hold zombies and peeked between the logs.

Emmy crawled up to crouch beside me, her beady eyes everywhere, able to see more in the light of the bonfire in the center of the camp.

The camp was basically a circle of sharpened logs around a circle of tents with spaces between them where clothes and supplies seemed to be stacked. Humans of all sizes roamed the camp, and armed guards were posted at the single entrance to the east.

"Connor?" Emmy whispered at me, anticipating what

I was already doing, running my eyes over every human in there for either my pet or Wally's.

"I don't see him, or his parents," I said, "though they could be in the tents."

Just then two of the humans walked up to the entrance from outside the camp, arms in the air.

"It's us."

"We can see that, Cathy. Did you get the bird?"

"Bird?" Emmy repeated, her eyes going wide.

"Might not be Pallas," I muttered, my eyes on the weapons the humans were carrying and a ring of keys hanging off one of the guard's belts. Humans used keys to open things. And lock things.

"Nah, too dark. A coyote might have snagged it while we were searching."

"Find bird first," Emmy declared, baring her teeth as if daring me to stop her.

I was the one who could see in the dark, so I led the way, retracing back in the direction we had seen the humans come.

We walked in a zig zag, left and right, left and right, Emmy calling for Pallas in a soft voice I'd never heard her use before. I alternated between looking at the ground and looking to the skies, still hoping to see our friend swooping down between the trees, unharmed and annoyed that we'd left our glade.

It was not to be. While we were still within sight of

the human's camp, we heard blubbering we recognized.

"Pallas!" Emmy declared, running straight into a hollow log where I heard her collide with something that cried out in pain.

I followed her in more carefully, seeing the pile of feathers and fur that were an owl and a hamster.

Emmy was running her paws all over the owl, squeaking and asking "Okay?" over and over again.

"Give the owl a second, Emmy!" I said, relieved to not have caused the death of this ridiculous bird. "Now, how badly are you hurt, Pal?"

Pal was still sobbing uncontrollably, so I directed my question at Emmy, who, against all odds, was the rational one of the pair.

"Do you feel any wounds, Emmy?"

Emmy raised her paws in front of me, which were clean. "Nothing."

"Thank the Saber," I said, sitting back on my haunches.

Emmy was petting the owl, humming to it softly, in almost a purr.

"You two stay here, I'm going back to the camp to look for Connor."

"No, wait, Pickles," Pal said in a watery voice. "I saw your friends."

"What?"

Pal took a deep steadying breath. "I'm sorry, the sound, it scared me …."

"Shhhh," said Emmy, continuing her ministrations.

"It's okay, Pal. The gunshot scared all of us," I said, trying to calm my hammering heart the way Emmy was calming this owl. "What did you see?"

"Your friends at the camp," Pal said. "I saw them."

"Alive?"

"Yes, alive, but Pickles …."

"Never mind. If they're alive, then Connor is probably there with them," I said excitedly, backing out of the log. "We just need to sneak into the camp …."

"No, you don't understand, Pickles. They are prisoners," Pal explained, following me out of the log.

"That's okay, we'll free them," I said, my tail out of the log now.

"There's more."

That stopped me at the mouth of the log. "What do you mean?"

Pal looked back at Emmy for encouragement, and she rubbed his back, nodding.

"They're in cages, Pickles," Pal answered finally. "The humans are going to eat them next."

"IT CAN'T BE true," I said for the fifth time. We had left the log and snuck to the edge of the camp, along the side of the fence where Pal said he saw the cages. The owl was walking on the ground with us and was even slower than the hamster. That wasn't fair since he could also fly, but it was very frustrating for me because the sun was starting to come up over the horizon and we were losing the advantage of stealth and surprise.

My mind kept bouncing between two possible truths: either Connor was here in this camp, or my friends were about to become dinner for these humans. They couldn't both be true at the same time. They just couldn't.

Emmy and Pal finally caught up to me, and the owl puffed out his chest, pointing between the logs. "There. Go through there."

Emmy nodded at me, and I slid between the logs to the boxes on the other side. I scratched at the first one. "Hannah," I hissed.

"Pickles?" asked Trip from inside the box I was scratching at.

"Yes," I hissed back.

"Pickles, I can't believe you came back for us," said Hannah's voice, the balm that I needed so badly.

"Of course I came for you," I said. "I will always find you."

Hannah started sniffing and I had to ask, "Are you okay?"

"Yeah, we're having a tea party in here, Pickles," said Wally's voice. "Ginger's wearing a crown and pretending to be one of the Queen's prized corgis."

"If that were true," Ginger's voice spoke out of the box, "I would be doing a truly fabulous job of it."

"This isn't funny," said Trip's voice.

I leaned against the box in relief. They were all fine.

"Now, could you get us out of here, please?" Trip said.

"Yes," I replied immediately, though I didn't have a plan as of yet. "What can you tell me about this box?"

"The sides are wood," Ginger said, "but the top has bars and we can see a latch with a lock."

The darkness was becoming less of a cover every second I delayed. "That's what the keys were for," I said to my friends. "I'll get the key. You, Emmy, and Pal come up with a distraction that we can launch when I get back."

"Who's Pal?" asked Wally.

I slid back through the logs and relayed the message to Pal and Emmy, leaving it to them to work out introductions and details with the rest of the fellowship.

Following the edges of the camp, I headed back the way we had come, looking for the guard I had seen earlier with the ring of keys. She wasn't at the gate anymore, and I couldn't see her in the camp itself. I was about to head back and grab Pal so he could do a more aerial search when I caught sight of her between the trees.

I sprinted after her, cursing the light that was starting to show as she walked away from the camp. Where was she going? I climbed a trunk and started to follow her that way, so that I was directly above her as she wove between trees. Finally, she seemed to find what she was looking for, and using a spade, she dug a shallow hole in the ground.

I finally understood what was going on: she was looking for a quiet place to litter. She took off her pants and hung them on a tree branch a couple steps away, squatting over the hole she had made. This was my chance.

I slid down the tree silently, an inch at a time. I could see the ring of keys. They were hooked onto a belt. Carefully, so carefully, I got my paws on the hook.

"How do you work this stupid thing?" I hissed under my breath, cursing my paws and applying my teeth instead. That didn't work either. Whatever the mechanism, I did not have the physical dexterity to get these keys off this belt. I glanced at the human. She seemed to be struggling with her morning litter, perhaps because she had altered her diet by eating cats and raccoons. Served her right.

The belt hung loose on the pants, so I grabbed the buckle and pulled it, backing up along the branch and dragging the belt through the belt loops. The keys jingled and I stopped, glancing down at the human, my mouth full of brass belt buckle. She hadn't noticed. I backed up again, slowly, so slowly until the belt was free of the pants.

"Hey!"

Not even bothering to look back, I climbed the tree, higher and higher, the buckle clamped in my teeth. Only when I was as high as I could go did I look back down to see the human pulling on her pants and cursing at me.

I would have laughed if that hadn't meant losing the keys, as she ran off towards the camp, yelling for help. As soon as she was gone, I leapt from tree to tree, lower and lower until I was running along the ground, the belt trailing behind me like a long tail, the keys jingling lightly along the ground. I had started to think about possible distractions when I heard yells go up from the camp.

"Fire!"

Fire? No way. I sprinted around the edge of the camp, dodging a zombie who had worked himself down to the ground while still impaled on a sharpened log.

Emmy and Pal were not where I had left them, but I suspected they were responsible for the panic on the other side of the camp where humans were now congregating. I leapt on top of the box, lowering the belt through the bars at the top.

"Here," I said. "Get Trip to open the lock, I don't know how. Get free and meet us ...."

I shrieked as someone grabbed me from behind, turning in mid-air to confront my attacker. It was a human, so I deployed claws on all four limbs, swiping and screeching and doing as much damage as I could.

The female had me securely by the scruff, but she squawked in response as my claw connected with her sensitive eye area, calling for help. Fortunately, the fire and the response to it meant it was just the two of us for now. My hide felt like it was being pulled from my skeleton, but I twisted and turned, trying to get free.

"Attack scenario Bravo!" yelled Wally from somewhere behind us, and I felt three bodies hit the human at the legs. With a scream, she tipped over, finally releasing my scruff.

"Let's go," I yelled, standing next to the human's head. I wasn't moving this time until I had seen all my friends to safety. Trip sprang away, bounding out towards the logs and shimmying his belly through, followed by Ginger and Wally. Emmy had already gone through and poked her head back to yell at us. Hannah shoved me towards the fence, but I still hadn't seen Pal. That's when he streaked over our heads, low enough to scare the human into a ball of fear. He led the way out of the camp, low to the ground and purring like a cat.

DAY THIRTY-ONE

We ran all the way to the stream on the east side of the camp. Wally wanted to cross it, to put the water between us and these humans, but Ginger pointed out that humans were better at crossing water than cats were, and we were more likely to lose someone to the current than deter our enemies.

Pal did another aerial pass while we found a small cave to hunker down in.

"No one is following," Pal said mid-air, coming in for a landing. He circled and tried to land at the mouth of the cave, but somehow miscalculated his speed and ended up rolling head over drumstick right into Trip.

Trip grabbed him in a hug in response. "Now,

someone needs to introduce us to our high flier here."

So, Emmy and I did just that, leaving out the abandon-ment story and cruel name, emphasizing his helpful nature and bravery. Pal glowed with our praise, but I could see his nocturnal schedule meant that he was starting to fade. We put together a simple nest for him in the back of the cave, and he fell asleep in minutes, snoring lightly with a hoot and a purr and a hoot and a purr.

"We'll turn him into a cat soon," Hannah said with a smile as we retreated to the front of the cave.

"Or a hamster," Emmy said, raising her chin in a challenge. Her whiskers were gone, burned away by her latest arsonist distraction, but she didn't look upset by it.

That made me laugh, something I hadn't done in a while. Probably not since the train had run through our group like a razor. Of course, that sobered me up. Think-ing about the train brought Connor front of mind again.

Wally had gone out for a quick hunt and was now carefully washing his paws in the stream, so Hannah and I walked out to him.

"Wally, did you see your pets or Connor at the camp?" I asked, voicing my worst fears and best hope at the same time. If Connor was there, then our quest was over, but it looked unlikely I could rejoin his family, since cats were now on the menu. I guess I couldn't hold that against them; a zombie apocalypse limited your options, and at the end of the day, cat meat was probably not that different from sheep meat, a staple of human diets. Plus, bags of cat food were scarce in an apocalypse, and I might have to start finding my meat sources in equally depressing ways. Or develop a taste for eating garbage like a raccoon.

Wally shook off the droplets of water. "No, they're not there, Pickles. I counted all twelve of the humans at that camp twice. I know I didn't miss them. There were no children at all, and my pets were not among the adults."

Emmy zoomed by, doing a wide circle pass on sentry duty.

"Slow it down, Emmy," Ginger advised as he and Trip emerged from the brush. They stuck their paws in the stream as well, washing off their meals. Trip waded into the water and gave himself a full body wash.

"Then we move on," I said, looking around at my fellowship. "I'm not sure how we pick up the trail again. Maybe we need to retrace our steps to before the net caught us."

"What?" I said as Wally and Hannah exchanged a similar wave of their tails that got my fur up.

It was Ginger who spoke, though. "Actually, we think we're still on the right trail, Pickles. These humans at the camp, they were talking about a safe house, and the people hiding out there."

"Well, that's … wonderful, isn't it?" I asked, glancing around at the faces of my friends, none of whom looked like this was the good news it sounded like.

"No, it's really not," said Trip, emerging from the stream like a furry well-rounded Aphrodite and moving to a considerate distance before shaking himself off.

"Why?" I pressed.

"Because they're planning to attack them, Pickles," Wally said, putting a paw on my shoulder. "If Connor and our pets are at the safe house, they are in grave danger."

Hannah curled around me for comfort. "These were the rejects, Pickles. The humans in the camp were banished by the humans at the safe house. Or at least some of them were. It wasn't entirely clear to me."

"Some of them were thrown out for being too violent, yes," Ginger agreed, "but some of them have never been in the safe house. I overheard one describing the layout of the house and its defenses to a new recruit last night."

"They plan to retake the safe house," Wally said, "and they have no qualms about killing everyone within to do it. This is a war, Pickles."

I wished he didn't seem so damn excited by it.

"Supposedly, it's a prime spot, with storehouses of food, and something called a greenhouse and a water supply of its own," Trip said, walking back towards us, his hair sticking up like a hedgehog.

"When is this attack supposed to happen?" I asked, my heart thudding dully.

"Tomorrow at dawn," said Emmy as she slowed down to join the discussion. "Fire won't stop them. They are ready. They are angry."

"So, what do we do?" I asked finally.

Everyone looked to Wally, his thick tail weaving and dancing as he thought.

"We could forge ahead, join our humans at the safe house and stand with them when the camp humans attack," Wally said, tracing a number "1" in the sand of the stream.

"We would have trouble warning them of the coming attack," Ginger said, "but at least we could rouse them before twilight. Cause a disturbance that gets them up."

Wally nodded as he traced a number "2." "Or we could attack these humans at the camp tonight, before sunrise. Reduce their numbers."

"I've never killed a human before," Trip said, raising his hand shakily. "Is it easy? It doesn't look easy."

We all shook our heads at him, except Emmy, who bared her teeth as if she could take them all herself.

"I don't think another fire is an option," Hannah said. "They will have taken measures after last night. And the hours before a battle would mean heightened security, would it not, Wally?"

I smiled. Wally was rubbing off on more than just me.

Wally nodded, slowly tracing a circle around the 1 and the 2 in the sand. "We could do some combination. Half of us warn the safe house humans, and half of us slow the efforts of these camp humans."

I nodded. This seemed like the best idea, and I watched the rest of the group slowly nod as well.

"Wally, you should lead the group to the safe house," I said, even though everything in me wanted to take the straightest, quickest path to lay eyes on Connor. "Your pets will recognize you and protect you, and you can help them prepare for the attack."

Wally agreed. "And you will lead the attack on the camp, Pickles?"

I looked to Emmy, who growled deep in her throat. "Emmy and I will attack the human camp at midnight. We will do our best to slow or stop the threat."

We spent the rest of the daylight alternating in shifts between eating and sleeping, though the nervous energy made it hard to do the latter.

I curled up with Hannah on a raised rock over the stream, the sunlight covering us in its warmth.

"Do you think Emmy will ever take a break?" she asked, her golden eyes half closed, her long lashes fluttering in the breeze.

I shook my head. That hamster never seemed to tire of her self-assigned guard duty. "Not unless we sit on her, which I'm seriously considering asking Trip to do."

Hannah snickered lightly, and my heart swelled. I was so lucky to be with her. So lucky to have found her.

"Have you thought about what we will do once you're with Connor again?" she asked.

"Sure, I think about it all the time," I answered, licking at her ears gently. "His family will take you in as well, I'm sure of it."

"You know I have bad luck with mammals."

"I know that you have good luck with these mammals," I replied.

She didn't argue the point, though I knew it was still an insecurity for her. "And you think Ginger and Emmy will find new pets among the safe house humans?"

"Surely," I said.

"And what about Trip and Pal?" she asked.

I looked down at Trip, who was arguing with Wally about something, waving his nimble black fingers to make a point. I think that annoyed Wally more. He hated not being the best at everything, and we heard his huffs of annoyance all the way up here on our rock.

"I don't see the humans taking a raccoon in, do you?" she asked.

"Maybe not," I admitted, "but he can still live with us at the safe house. Like he did in the city, before all this happened."

"He lived with a family," she corrected. "A gaze of other raccoons. Now he would be alone. Like Pallas.

Neither of them is an indoor animal. They won't like to be kept indoors," she said, yawning before closing her eyes and falling asleep in my arms.

"That doesn't seem right, does it?" I whispered, mostly to myself, thinking about my fellowship, and my responsibility for bringing them all together like this. Could I really abandon Pallas and Trip to a lonely and perhaps dangerous life outside the safe house?

I was still mulling this over as the sun reached its zenith in the sky.

Wally and Ginger jumped up on to the rock, the older cat speaking in low tones. "Pickles, it's time for my team to head out. We want to give ourselves enough time to access the safe house and assess its inner workings."

I nodded as Hannah stirred. We had discussed her part in the action, and though she didn't like it, she was going with Wally and Ginger. Three cats were more likely to be welcomed into the safe house than a raccoon, a hamster, and an owl.

"If no attack comes before daybreak," Ginger said, "we will assume you were successful, and expect your arrival at the safe house."

"But if you don't show up …," Hannah said, her worry written in the movement of her whiskers.

"Then I'll expect you to come find us," I said with a smile.

Ginger walked up and scented me. "Be careful, but

be ferocious. I want a tale I can tell my grand-kittens. And keep that mad hamster out of trouble."

I grinned. "And you try and watch over these two."

Wally nodded. "I'll give you a moment to say your goodbyes then, Pickles. Good luck."

He jumped down from the rock, closely followed by Ginger.

"You'll be careful?" I asked Hannah, nose to nose with her.

"I will if you will," she replied. "No undue heroics. Okay?"

"Agreed," I said.

We climbed down together, and she followed Wally and Ginger out of the camp, glancing back at me until they were in the trees.

Trip came up and slung an arm around me. "Emmy finally went down for a nap, but I had to promise we'd cover her sentry duty together."

I sighed, and we started a small circle around the cave area.

"Trip, Hannah said something that got me thinking," I said as Trip dug a worm out of the ground and sucked it back with a satisfied slurp. "You're not really an indoor animal."

"Nope, not my bag," Trip replied. "Dammit, my bag. Those humans made me drop it. I'd forgotten about that till now."

"And Pallas, well, he's an owl. He would not deal well with being locked inside a safe house," I continued as we rounded the circuit, heading back towards the stream.

"Ha! No, he would not," Trip agreed, then he stopped suddenly. "Wait. Are you talking about ... you're going to live with Connor in the safe house?"

I stopped too, kicking at a root. "Well, yeah, that was always the plan. To rejoin my ... family."

"Oh," Trip said, starting to walk again, his tail dragging along the ground uncharacteristically.

"I'm not saying it's the way it has to be — a lot has changed," I said, following him. "I'm starting to realize that your family can be more than one thing. You and Pal are family. I can love more than one mammal. I *do* love more than one mammal. But we need to ...."

Trip stopped again, suddenly.

"Trip?"

He pointed a black paw towards the stream where a single zombie was struggling through the current towards us.

"Trees," I said, pushing Trip towards the nearest one. We climbed quickly, but the zombie continued its march, rising out of the stream on all fours, mouth gnashing.

"He's headed for the cave!" Trip said, scampering from tree to tree. "What do we do, Pickles?"

I had no idea, but he wasn't going to hurt my sleeping friends within. We landed on the tree branch closest to the cave as the zombie crawled towards it, and I looked around desperately for something to stop his forward movement.

"Hey! Dead guy!" Trip yelled at the zombie. "Up here brainless!"

The zombie's head swung up our way, and I thought maybe Trip had done it, but then we heard a terrified hoot from within the cave. The zombie refocused on the prey he could reach, his head disappearing into the mouth of the cave.

"NO!" I yelled, launching myself into the air and landing on the zombie's back.

The zombie lurched up at the sound and suddenly I was claw deep in this monster's back, holding on for dear life, my front paws digging into his shoulders. He turned left and right, looking for me, seemingly not understanding that I was attached to him. What had I done?

"Pickles!" Trip called from the tree above.

"Get them out, Trip!" I yelled back, causing the zombie to start twisting again, looking for the source of the meows. He stumbled towards the stream and, instinctively, I pulled with my left paw. To my surprise, he turned, my claws in his shoulders directing him left. A plan started to form in my head, and I pulled left again. The zombie turned left again, groaning but still moving forward at my direction. He built up speed, moving into the trees.

Above me, a familiar figure swooped.

"Pal!" I yelled, causing the zombie to stop and look around again. "I have an idea!"

"THIS IS THE maddest plan you've ever hatched," Trip said from the shadows where we were observing the camp. He was pulling at his whiskers so hard I was worried he'd be left with none by the end of the night.

"Brilliant, not mad," corrected our equally mad hamster, who was sharpening her claws on a rock nearby.

"I think it's a little of both," I admitted, nervously looking at the three zombies impaled in front of us. They still seemed to have energy, which was key to this plan.

Above us, a hoot signaled Pal's landing and Trip extended his paws to slow the owl's descent. Pallas tumbled to a stop right in front of us, and Emmy picked him up and dusted him off.

"They're awake, and ready. I think they're minutes away from making their move," Pallas said, out of breath from his mission. "They're taking down part of the fence on the other side."

"Then that's where we need to get to," I said, moving forward, feeling my legs shaking and reminding myself that this was MY harebrained idea. "The one on the left looks like she needs the least effort. Emmy, you should take her."

Emmy nodded, glaring at her target.

"Trip, are you sure you can do this?" I repeated, looking at his paws as they pulled at his whiskers.

"I don't like it, but yes, I can do it," he said, dropping his whiskers self-consciously.

"Stealth is going to be key, but so is ruthlessness," I said, grabbing Emmy by the scruff. I climbed the tree we had picked and walked out onto the branch with her in my mouth. I put her down cautiously on the stem in front of me, and she silently bared her sparkling teeth in anticipation.

With the silence of a ninja, she dropped onto the back of the zombie, claws extended. The zombie didn't even notice, proving once and for all that it wasn't smell or touch that they used to track their prey. It was some combination of sight and sound. I took a deep breath and leapt onto the next zombie, fixing my claws into its large shoulders, and then nodded up at Trip. He jumped … and slid right down the back of the zombie to land with a thud on the ground.

All three zombies noticed and turned to look down at the confused raccoon with groans of displeasure. I used my left claw to turn my zombie back, hissing at Trip. "Try again!"

Meanwhile, Emmy was slowly working her zombie off its skewer. Left claw, right claw, left claw, right claw. Pal zoomed around behind the zombies, hooting softly so that they focused on him and moved backwards off the logs.

Emmy freed her zombie first and gave a hoot of her own, then charged off into the woods. I would have called her back, but Pallas suddenly shot off into the camp.

"Pallas!" I called instead.

"Ooof!" said Trip, landing on the ground behind his zombie again.

"Trip, Pal just flew off. What's going on?" I asked, still working my zombie off its log, starting to sweat at the effort.

Trip climbed the tree for the third time, squinting into the camp. "They're leaving! Pickles, the humans are leaving!"

Desperation made us work faster. I got my zombie free just as Emmy rode her zombie back to us, its arms extended like the Frankenstein's monster I'd seen in a TV movie. "Come on!" she yelled.

"Trip, follow us on foot!" I said, turning my zombie to follow Emmy's, skirting the edge of the camp and following the humans. Pallas flew back our way, hooting in alarm.

"They're running towards the safe house, Pickles.

You have to hurry."

My paws strained against my zombie, pulling his muscles so that we followed the owl through the twilight, ignoring the hamster who was squealing her delight at her ride, making her zombie turn spasmodically to locate the source of the sound.

I was tempted to chastise her, but the sound of my voice would only make my zombie look for me as well, so I only gritted my teeth instead.

Ahead, I could see the group of humans running towards the safe house, which I could also see in the distance. It too was ringed with sharpened logs, but the lights seemed dim. Had Wally succeeded in rousing the humans within?

I turned my zombie left so that I could come at the humans from that side, hoping Emmy would understand she should attack from the other side.

We were close enough to the safe house that I could see the structure inside: a large cement building with floodlights on the roof and barbed wire around the edges. The attacking humans were moving slower now, edging their way to an unguarded part of the fence that seemed to be under repair.

No matter what I did, I couldn't get my zombie to move faster, and he didn't seem to have sighted the humans at all, so I was constantly directing him back towards the safe house. My arms were so tired I considered leaping off my ride and attacking the humans directly, especially when one of them lit a branch and tossed it over the fence. I wouldn't have lasted a minute, though, even with all of Wally's training.

That's when the floodlights came on, all focused on the humans of the camp.

There were yells from within the safe house compound. Wally had done it!

I was close enough to see the faces of the camp humans now, confused and livid that their attack had gone awry. More importantly, my zombie was charging towards them without any prompting from me.

The humans finally saw us and screamed in terror as my zombie and I attacked. It must have been a sight: a dead human barreling towards them, steered by a cat on its back. Whatever I looked like, the hamster version must have looked even crazier. I heard Emmy before I saw her, coming in from my right as the humans hacked at my zombie. They were trying to defend themselves, but were now being struck by our zombies from both sides. I retracted my claws and leapt off my zombie ride, streaking towards Emmy and climbing up her dead human like a ladder.

"Can't get ... free!" she hissed, and I grabbed her paw and pulled at it. She was well stuck.

"Duck!" she yelled and thankfully, I listened, ducking as a human decapitated her zombie with a sword. The zombie fell backwards, and I wrapped myself around Emmy's struggling body as we hit the ground, trapping us under its body.

"Mmmph," I said, squished under the two-hundred-pound zombie, unable to move. "Emmy?"

Emmy was free from her zombie, but she was unconscious in my paws.

Somewhere above us I could hear a loud hooting sound. Pallas had joined the fray.

"Hold on, Emmy," I said, twisting and turning, trying to work my way free of the lifeless body on top of us. My right paw dug in the dirt, my left paw was firmly wrapped around Emmy, and then I felt something grab my right paw.

"Ack!" I screamed, sure we were done for this time.

"Pickles," said a voice I recognized, and I stopped fighting against the paw, allowing Trip to drag us out from under our dead weight.

"Get her to safety!" I said to Pallas, holding Emmy up to the skies. Pal scooped the hamster up and flew towards the boundary of the safe house, rising up and down as he flew because he was having so much trouble with the weight.

Trip and I dodged falling body parts and screaming humans as they poured out of the compound, closely followed by cats I knew and loved.

"Pickles," called Wally. "This way."

I sprinted towards Hannah and Ginger, Trip close at my tail.

"Get inside! The humans can handle this," Wally said, directing the attack from a raised platform of boxes. We leapt up beside him, pulling Trip up as well when he struggled to climb the side. First chance I got I planned to properly sharpen the claws of my raccoon friend.

"Pallas!" he called, waving at the owl who looked done in at the effort of carrying a senseless hamster.

I didn't think they would make it, but somehow, Pal did it, dropping like a stone onto the raised platform. Trip cradled Emmy in his arms, I tucked Pal between Hannah and me, and we all stared down at the human battle below.

It wasn't pretty. The zombies we had rode into the skirmish had done their damage, several of the camp humans wailing at bites to their necks or arms that meant their lives were over. Wally continued to yell encouragement at the humans, looking more proud than a mother corgi in the British Royal Family. The safe house humans surrounded their peers, in numbers that tripled their enemies, but still more than a few refused to surrender and needed to be put down. I turned my face away from the carnage, squeezing Pal harder at my side, and met the eyes of the one mammal I had fought so hard to find.

"Pickles?" asked the sweet voice of my pet. My Connor.

His eyes the warm brown I saw in my dreams, his cheeks less full than last time I saw him.

He was pointing at me from his mother's arms, reaching for me with his little hands, when I nodded at him and he realized he was right. I was his Pickles. His mother did a double-take, running her eyes over the motley crew of animals sitting on a platform above the mayhem below. And then I was in my Connor's arms, squeezed so tight I could barely breathe and loving every wonderful second of it.

DAY ONE

That first day was a blur of reunions and explanations as my small fellowship was integrated into the safe house population. I was determined to keep this family together, no matter what it took, but I needn't have worried, because my pet had room in his heart for all of us.

Connor introduced the whole fellowship by name to the humans of the compound, relaying our acts of bravery in his limited toddler words. As Wally explained it, youngling mammals were less burdened by the realities of the world, and therefore able to listen and hear the animals around them. As a small animal, he understood about half of what I said to him, and as he grew older, less and less.

That meant that the adult humans around him understood about an eighth of what he managed to communicate, but I didn't care. The important thing was that when one of the adult humans made a move towards Trip, Connor, understanding his responsibility to my fellowship, threw his arms around the raccoon, and told them he loved him, so they'd better not hurt him.

I could have cried at his loyalty (I think I might have, in fact, shed a tear), and it was a successful strategy for so young a human. Trip looked around at the staring adults and gently returned the hug, eliciting "aws!" from the audience. He had won them over.

Wally discovered that one of his pets was lost on their journey to the safe house. He took it very hard, becoming even more protective of the human female still in his charge. He took responsibility for communicating Pal's and Trip's needs to his female, with Connor and I as influencers. She was a good human, and within a week, she had started to build a small off-shoot loft that led from the compound into a tree where Trip and Pal could come and go as they pleased without fear of zombie attacks.

We called our little home "The Menagerie," and it became the place where all of us would gather in the evening to share our stories. I still put Connor to bed —

that would always be my job — but I spent the wee hours with the rest of my family sharing food and laughter.

Hannah was literally fought over, which didn't surprise me at all. Two teenage girls were both dying to become her new charge, begging their parents to claim her services. Hannah was flattered by the attention and made the decision herself, choosing to spend half her time with each of the girls. My Abyssinian love was finally changing her own luck and beginning to trust other mammals again. Connor created a little fort out of his own precious blankie for the two of us in our cat house, affording us a little privacy, understanding in his own way that this was the cat I would spend the rest of my life with.

Ginger became the roaming tomcat of the compound, impressing everyone with his ability to alert them to both danger and promise, going on patrol with whoever was on guard duty. I watched him walk the battlements at the foot of a well-armed guard, and he would wink at me reminding me he was still the wise-cracking tabby at heart.

And Emmy? She was carried into the medical room, an anxious owl hooting and flying above, but she would not wake. We dug her a small grave with our paws, and the humans carved her name into a wooden tombstone.

We — the remaining fellowship — stood over her grave, our hearts heavy at the loss.

"What we need here is a reveille," Wally said, looking around as if a trumpet would present itself, along with a mammal with the fingers to play such an instrument. When none appeared, Wally took the bronze star off his collar and carefully laid it on the grave.

"Should we say something?" Trip said, wiping at his masked eyes.

"She was the best hamster I ever met," said Ginger. "I'll never forget how she saved that baby chipmunk. She changed me that day. I wouldn't be the cat I am today without her."

We nodded solemnly, and then Wally's face broke out in a rare smile. "I'll never forget how mad she was when the chipmunks grabbed us in that treehouse."

We laughed. "Mad was her default setting," I murmured, hugging Hannah close.

"Not to me," said Pallas in his deep voice. "She was nothing but loving to me. From the moment I met her."

Pallas burst into tears and Trip took one look at him and did the same. They collapsed into each other's arms and seemed to be competing for who could be the noisiest. Soon the two of them were bawling loud enough to attract zombies.

"Okay, shh, okay," Ginger said, glancing up at the guards on duty who were now staring down at the spectacle. "Pull it together, mammals."

I couldn't tell if he was embarrassed by the display or

worried about zombie attacks. Possibly a little of both.

"Pickles," Wally said.

"I know," I said, leaning towards the weeping animals. "Trip. Pal ...."

"No, Pickles, look!" said Wally, pointing at the little grave. The dirt on top was moving, the general's star shaking its way off the top of the mound.

"What?" Hannah exclaimed, her back arching in response.

"Bugs. It's just bugs," sniffed Pal, his huge eyes growing wider.

In our defense, we didn't freak out until a small pink paw poked out through the dirt.

"Zombie hamster!" Trip yelled, tripping over his own feet in his effort to get away. He grabbed Pal and started pushing us all back towards the main house. I think if he had had his precious plastic bag at that moment, he would have tossed us all in it and sprinted to safety like a furry, masked Santa Claus.

"Where?" sputtered zombie Emmy, spitting dirt in every direction as she rose from her own grave.

"Can zombie hamsters talk?" Hannah asked, pushing back against Trip's frantic movements.

Zombie Emmy snorted, more dirt flying out of her nose. "Zombies can't talk."

I stepped forward, and both Wally and Ginger grabbed my tail. "Emmy?"

"Yes?" she replied, still rubbing dirt from her face. "Where zombie hamster? I'd see it."

I threw my arms around her. "You're not dead!"

"Not dead," she confirmed. "Playing dead. Fine. Hungry."

She stooped to pick up the bronze star and bit into it, testing the metal before looking up at us curiously. Wally looked thunderously angry, his mouth gaping, but Ginger and Hannah burst into peals of laughter. Trip tiptoed towards her, gobsmacked, but it was Pal who had the most unpredictable reaction, fainting right where he stood, his spindly legs sticking straight up in the air. Trip gathered up the owl with a sigh and all seven of us trooped back into The Menagerie, our laughter filling the air, our arms around each other.

ACKNOWLEDGEMENTS

Like most books, this one would not have made it out of my notebooks but for some awesome mammals around me. First, a big thank you to my little family for putting up with my time away from them to create Pickles' world and for being subjected to several rounds of beta reading.

Barry Jowett, my editor at DCB, you are a patient, lovely man, and I appreciate all the work you put into my manuscript.

Emma Dolan is the illustrator who can seemingly take any story I write, be it a 1930s detective or a zombie-fighting cat, and translate it into the most beautiful cover on the bookshelf. I am endlessly grateful to have you in my publishing life.

My little writing group, who have been forced to listen to the exploits of my rag-tag bunch of adventurers for years, Joyce Grant, Alisha Sevigny, Colleen Ross, Bev Katz and Heather Jackson, thank you!

To the indie bookstores like Book City on St. Clair W and the Mysterious Bookshop in NYC, who continue to carry my books and speak of my characters to your readership, thank you!

Thank you to the Ontario Arts Council for their repeated support of this series, and to Karen Li for being the first to support and guide Pickles on her journey. And a shout-out to my teacher, Kathy Kacer who helped me make the transition from YA to middle-grade author.

To my first editor, Kat Kruger, who continues to be a huge source of support and love, thank you.

Huge thanks to Shelagh Rogers and Marc Côté for your kind faith and support.

And finally, I must dedicate this book to all the four-legged animals who have called me pet over the years, Princess, Gauss, Mendel, Darwin, Guttenberg, and Copernicus.

Angela Misri is an author and journalist of Indian descent. She was born in London, U.K. and briefly lived in Buenos Aires before moving to Canada  in 1982. Angela is the author of the Portia Adams Adventures series and several essays on Sherlock Holmes. She earned her BA in English Literature from the University of Calgary and her MA in Journalism from the University of Western Ontario. As a former CBC Radio digital manager and the Digital Director at *The Walrus*, Angela is never offline (although she prefers to write long form in notebooks). Angela plays MMORPGs, speaks several web languages, and owns too many comic books. She currently lives in Toronto, ON.

We acknowledge the sacred land on which Cormorant Books operates. It has been a site of human activity for 15,000 years. This land is the territory of the Huron-Wendat and Petun First Nations, the Seneca, and most recently, the Mississaugas of the Credit River. The territory was the subject of the Dish With One Spoon Wampum Belt Covenant, an agreement between the Iroquois Confederacy and Confederacy of the Ojibway and allied nations to peaceably share and steward the resources around the Great Lakes. Today, the meeting place of Toronto is still home to many Indigenous people from across Turtle Island. We are grateful to have the opportunity to work in the community, on this territory.

We are also mindful of broken covenants and the need to strive to make right with all our relations.